Mania

At The

Mainframe

by

Paul Tidy

In memory of Tony, a lifelong friend

Introduction

In the 1980s the bigger companies operated large mainframe computers capable of much faster data processing in less time. These computers were usually run seven days a week by staff working a three-shift pattern: days, evenings and nights. The shift-workers were usually young, educated to A level standard and keen to work overtime if required.

In those days the workplace social scene was in full swing: a few pints at lunchtime and after work was almost obligatory. Some companies had a bar, restaurant and regular teams for football, darts and many other activities. Health & Safety did exist but was generally ignored by anyone under forty-five.

Associated Media Operations had been run from a side street in a busy part of Central London since the company was established in 1961. Over the course of the intervening years, AMO had expanded until, eventually, the surrounding properties in the street had also been purchased by the business for its own use.

The firm's computer department was now based here with each shift usually manned by twelve computer operators.

Chapter 1

Count Basie's Boys

It was 10.30 Friday night, and several cars were jostling to turn into the no through road. At the end of the cul-de-sac was a large building with a sign saying *Associated Media Operations, Sulcrem House*. As the convoy of cars approached the security gates to the side of the building, a loud groan came from Ivan, the security man. Although this was a busy part of London he always felt uneasy as the night shift approached.

A shape got out of the first car. It was a large gorilla, with a security pass in one hand and a banana in the other.

"Evening Ivan," it said in a loud London accent.

Now Ivan was about six feet one, well built, still pretty fit for his sixty years, but he was taken by surprise by this twenty stone primate.

"It's only me, Dennis. Look, I've got my pass."

"Well, you don't look like the photo. I mean it should say 'Guy the Gorilla', not Dennis," replied Ivan.

Ivan felt a bit calmer and started to relax when, out of the other cars, emerged Idi Amin, Donald Duck, Clint Eastwood, a dolphin, and the front and rear ends of a horse.

A gun fired blanks, and loud quacks and horse noises rang out. Dennis, legs bowed, leapt onto his car and began to beat his chest with his fists.

"Stop it. Stop it." yelled Ivan, now quite annoyed. "Get those cars parked or I'll ring the police."

One by one the vehicles went through the gates amid laughter and car horns tooting. Yes, the night shift had arrived.

In the recreation room some members of staff were playing pool, drinking coffee, smoking and watching TV.

"Here comes trouble." said Glen, an operator on the evening shift, breaking away from the Muppets' video for a split second.

As the car park backed on to their rest room, members of the evening shift had all heard what was going on outside. Looking out through the window briefly and laughing, then returning to their activities as if nothing had happened. This sort of thing was quite common on the night shift.

It was still about twenty minutes from the time when the shifts switched over. The car park fell silent as, in through reception, walked some animals, a cowboy and an African dictator.

"Have you lot been to *Count Basie's* again?" asked Norman, the evening shift leader. He had been to *Count Basie's* many times himself and knew Friday night was daft costume night. It was a small, but lively pub just down the main road, close enough to walk to and stagger back from.

"No, we've been to the Conservative Club, Norman," Idi Amin replied.

As laughter rang out once more, the boys from the fancy dress soirée at *Count Basie's* went to change in the locker room.

Idi Amin had transformed into Charlie, a tall, lean West Indian: Donald Duck turned into Stuart, the leader of the night shift, a small and opinionated bearded individual who kept fish. It was rumoured that when hungry he filled a saucepan with water, stole two or three fish out of the tank and boiled them for a few minutes to enjoy in a toasted sandwich. It was never proven, though.

On the floor of the locker room a large blue dolphin wriggled like mad.

"Get me out of 'ere." it shouted.

In a matter of seconds, after some help, Flipper had emerged as Rick, a large, ginger haired male who was rumoured to have more beer in his system than blood.

Clint Eastwood looked at the gorilla and asked, "Say honey, do I know your sister?"

The gorilla said nothing. But, an instant later, he flung his arms around Clint, pushing him to the floor, then picked him up and ran off with him.

Out in the street, on the other side of the building, Mr Patel was just leaving his newsagent's shop when he spotted a twenty stone gorilla running past, carrying a cowboy. He scratched his head and said to himself, "This area is getting stranger all the time."

In the computer room the evening shift was almost finished. At the operating console stood Gordon. He was of medium build, with a moustache that would make any latter-day dictator proud, and a condescending attitude towards his colleagues. He looked at his watch.

"Come on, come on, where are they?" he said impatiently.

He did not like the night shift much since the previous month, when they had tied him to a chair and left him gagged outside the bank. When the police had discovered him the following morning he was wearing a traffic cone on his head, put there by some passers-by during the night. Gordon had threatened to tell the management about the incident, but didn't know exactly who had been involved. Fortunately for Charlie and Stuart, the camera flashlight had temporarily blinded Gordon and by the time he could see properly again, all he could recognize were the front doors of the bank.

Hurriedly and out of breath, Dennis stepped out of the gorilla suit in the locker room. Beside him, Clint Eastwood transformed into Jeff, a short, stocky, tough, blond, Spurs supporter. Next to him were the front and back of a spotted horse. Pulling off the head was Bruce, tall and strong with spikey blond hair; slipping out of the back legs was a red-faced, short, dark-haired, lad called Tim.

All members of the shift were under thirty-five except Stuart who was forty-two. Most of them had worked together for at least ten years. The money was good, the work was easy, but more importantly, they had a good laugh on every shift. Day shifts could be less fun due to the presence of the managers. At night though, the hours of silliness reigned.

As the clock approached 10.55 a group of eleven noisy, casually dressed, but lively individuals burst through the doors of the computer room. In the middle of them Charlie bobbed up and down excitedly. Stereo music blared out from the ghetto blaster on his shoulder and a loud cheer went up from the evening shift: they would be going home quite soon.

"Is there much 'appening?" Stuart asked, as Norman started to explain the evening's problems, but before he had said three words Stuart said,

"Right, get lost then."

Norman looked startled but turned and said,

"See you boys."

Eleven fairly sensible lads followed Norman out of the room and the evening shift was over.

Chapter 2

Clumsy Eugene

Ivan mumbled goodnight then listened as the sound of car engines revving filled the car park. A small green sports car seemed to be making more noise and smoke than the rest. One by one the evening shift's cars sped their way homeward. All except the green one. Ivan could see the back wheels turning on their own, but the car was not moving. He went over to offer help.

From inside the stubborn vehicle, shouting and swearing could be heard. It was Brian, the evening shift's practical joker. Only last week he had put a smoke bomb under Dennis's car after he had just parked it. The result had been hilarious as Dennis and Ivan ran around with a fire extinguisher trying to stop what they thought was a dangerous situation.

"Hang on, I'll give you a push," said Ivan.

As he pushed, Brian revved up hard then, all of a sudden, the car gave a bump and, with a loud wheel spin took off, leaving Ivan sprawled across the ground. It was all Brian could do to avoid the gates and stop about a foot from the other side of the building.

From a second storey window, very loud laughter could be heard. All eleven members of the night shift, including Charlie, who had a video camera recording the whole thing, were falling about laughing, unable to be discreet any longer. Dennis had got his revenge.

With a two-fingered gesture in the direction of the second floor, Brian sped off.

"Which one of you morons owns this car jack?" shouted Ivan to the sounds of even more laughter.

The computer room was a state of the art, multi-million pound area the size of half a football pitch. It consisted of many large and smaller square shapes ranging from the size of a telephone box to a washing machine. Some contained magnetic tape decks on which were loaded the computer tapes, some housed large data-holding disc drives. The various data-processing cabinets were in constant use. The sides of the room were lined with large printers and boxes of stationery.

There were adjoining rooms which contained the computer library, with a vast array of information from various departments of the firm. At the centre of this temple of technology was the central console where all the work was scheduled. It was an immaculately clean, air-conditioned, professional environment. Visitors to the site marvelled at how well run it was and how they had enjoyed the daytime tour. If only they knew how different it was at night.

As they returned to the computer room they each went to their various workstations. Some would load tapes and some would take large volumes of computer print to be sorted. They all knew exactly what to do.

In a separate room, three machines extracted the carbon paper from between the sheets of computer paper and punched the holes at the side of the special prints. It was in this room that Eugene worked.

Small, short-haired Eugene, with a big stomach and the facial expression of a bag of flour. One thing separated Eugene from the rest: not only was he about as much use as a chocolate tea pot but trouble always found him, or he found it. He was called Jonah by the shift for obvious reasons.

Three weeks previously he had had a lucky escape when a parcel was delivered by a huge lorry driver wearing dark glasses.

"Look, it's Ray Charles," Eugene had said.

The driver had said nothing, but waited for the signature on his delivery sheet which confirmed the parcel had arrived safely and undamaged. He was just standing there whistling when Eugene continued,

"No, it's not Ray Charles, it's Stevie Wonder."

Eugene had then started swaying, singing and pretending to play the electric organ. A large hand had tried to slip underneath the small hole in the glass surround of the reception area. Eugene squealed and stepped back hurriedly.

"I wear these because I have an eye problem. Now you're gonna have one."

The van driver made grabbing movements and each time he did Eugene stepped back another pace.

"Help. Help." he cried out, then turned and sprinted to the computer room.

"What's up Jonah?" asked Dennis, still looking at the main computer screen.

"There's a bloke trying to do me in at reception," Eugene's voice was shaky.

Dennis immediately pulled a £10 note from his pocket and said,

"'Ere, give 'im this from me."

"No, please help me. I'm scared."

Still trembling, Eugene took three more paces towards Dennis. Without looking up, Dennis pressed 27 on his intercom. From the other end of the intercom came a startled shout and a loud noise, then a groan. He had woken Ivan up with a start.

"Hello, Security," came the groggy voice.

"Eugene's done it again. Can you sort it out Ivan please?" said Dennis. He then explained the story that Eugene had told him.

"That boy's a pain in the neck," said Ivan.

"We know," replied Dennis.

"Leave it with me," Ivan said in a military manner.

Eugene watched from a distance as Ivan and the van driver walked from the delivery entrance to the van. The man was waving his arms about irately. As a last gesture, the driver took off his dark glasses and showed Ivan his eyes. Ivan patted him on the shoulder and nodded.

Eugene breathed a sigh of relief as he saw the van finally drive away, thinking to himself,

"I wonder why he hates Stevie Wonder so much."

This particular shift, Stuart instructed Eugene to make tea and coffee ready for the first break of the evening. He had a good ten to fifteen minutes to do this as half the shift wouldn't be in the rest room until one o'clock. The tea, coffee and sugar were kept in large square plastic containers on top of the fridge. Eugene started to make preparations for the first break. Six cups in a line, kettle on. Just as he had opened the fridge door to get the milk, he remembered he had left one of his machines running. After racing out of the well-equipped kitchen he turned the corner, only to bump into Tim who was carrying two armfuls of computer tapes. Both parties fell to the ground.

"Sorry," said Eugene.

"It could only be you, Jonah, couldn't it?" sighed Tim.

Eugene helped with the tapes then, walking quickly, he carried on into the paper handling room and turned off his machine. Again, almost running, he returned to the kitchen but as he did so, collided with the open fridge door. The next thing he knew the fridge was upturned and its contents scattered. The open tea, coffee and sugar boxes from the top of the fridge spilled onto the floor. Rick had an open bottle of home brew in the fridge. This, combined with the

9

milk, some mayonnaise, yoghurt, broken eggs, and fruit made a mess worthy of a chimps' tea party. Tea bags were strewn across the rapidly forming sea of grunge over the kitchen floor. At one end of the mess was Eugene, with the fridge jackknifed across the floor.

"Help. Help." he cried, vaguely recalling the same words from three weeks previously.

Tim, who had gone to investigate the cries for help, laughed when he saw the scene before him. But when he realised that it was made up of the shift's food supply, he decided they had to be told at once.

One by one the boys looked at the scene of devastation. They huddled into a group outside the kitchen and Stuart said,

"Right, no tea, no coffee, no food thanks to Eugene. It's a mess in there, lads." Then a smile spread over his face. "Fetch the reception chair please Bruce, oh and lots of Sellotape."

"Right ho," said Bruce and off he went. Stuart put his head round the kitchen door and said to Eugene,

"Don't worry, we'll sort you out."

"Thanks lads," said Eugene, relieved they weren't angrier.

Bruce arrived with the chair and tape.

"I think Eugene needs cleaning up – a wash in fact." Stuart was grinning evilly.

Stuart handed out the tape and knew he didn't have to say any more. They all walked into the kitchen and picked up Eugene who was quite overwhelmed by his colleagues' care and attention. They put him into the chair and Eugene appreciated how they had bothered to sit him down in case he had hurt himself. It wasn't until six different rolls of tape had been repeatedly wrapped around his ankles, shins, thighs, arms, and chest that he started to worry.

Eugene could hear water running in the toilet block. Then, as if he were the Pope in his sedan chair, he was lifted aloft and carried towards the sound of the running water. The shower curtains were pulled back to reveal the water gushing out on full. Gently placing him under the running water ten voices then started a repetitious rendering of 'I'm Singing in the Rain'. The song grew fainter as the boys walked out leaving Eugene and the cold shower together.

The reception door opened and Ivan entered on his first check of the night. It was one of several checks he was supposed to make. Shouting and agonised cries greeted him, but before he could get to the source of the noise, Rick approached with two large bottles in his hands.

"Try this homebrew of mine Ivan," he said as he thrust the beer at him. Before Ivan could say anything, Rick said,

"But be careful, it makes you deaf."

"That strong is it?" asked Ivan, smiling. "Who's in there?" he asked, pointing towards the toilet block.

"It's Eugene," said Rick with a downcast look, thinking Ivan was going to get them all into trouble.

"Eugene, you say? Right." Ivan turned, walked towards the reception door, stopped and shouted across to Rick,

"Can't hear a word." With that he shut the door and returned to the security office.

Five minutes later Stuart, Dennis, Tim and Bruce returned to the toilet block and switched off the shower.

"Go home and change and bring back some supplies or don't come back," said Stuart in a commanding tone.

"I can't get in my car like this," said Eugene.

"Well, walk home then," said Stuart.

With this the four of them left Eugene dripping all over the floor, mumbling obscenities to himself. As he made for the outside door, he wondered why the lads were so hard on him. He didn't realise it was because they considered him a complete waste of space.

Gingerly squelching past a sniggering Ivan, Eugene made for his car. He didn't have too far to go and would be home in ten minutes. At the four-bedroomed semi, mum, dad and his younger sister would all be asleep. If he was quiet, he could change, get the milk, tea and coffee and be back at work within half an hour without any of them knowing he'd been home.

Meanwhile, back in the computer room kitchen a clear up operation was underway. Charlie had salvaged some dry tea bags and some milk. When the floor was clear he switched on the kettle again.

After they had their tea and were back at their specific work areas they let the rest of the shift have their break. This would be repeated throughout the night at hourly intervals.

Standing in the cleaned up kitchen were the three other shift members: Ben, a stocky sociopath, short and with an even shorter fuse, he never backed down from any form of argument or skirmish, Ravi, a plump, hirsute Asian, and Juan, a Spaniard with an average build and a tendency to muddle his English words. As they waited for the tea to brew, they chatted.

"Why didn't you go to *Count Basie's* earlier?" Ravi asked.

"I had my Inglees lethon with my cousin," answered Juan.

"Yeah, I couldn't go 'cos I had a spot of car trouble," Ben pitched in.

"Oh, you car no go? I get Barry, he feex it," said Juan, helpfully.

Barry was his friend from the day shift who was a wizard with cars.

"My car's all right, but I was forced to damage someone else's," said Ben.

Frowning, he told his version of events.

Waiting at the traffic lights in his BMW a Porsche had cut him up. Not wanting to look silly, Ben had given chase and cut the Porsche driver up. At the next set of lights the Porsche driver had got out of his car and Ben had got out of his BMW. Being about six feet to Ben's five, the taller man had felt immediately superior and, stupidly took off his jacket. Ben grinned, then snarled and, as he stepped towards his opponent, a large iron bar dropped from his sleeve to his hand. On seeing this the Porsche driver's superior expression changed to one of horror. He ran back to his car and locked it. But this didn't deter Ben. He just attacked the car instead. He hit the roof, the bonnet, the boot, all in less than a minute. Viewing the scene in his mirror as he drove off, Ben left a very sick-looking car and driver behind him.

"Well, he asked for it didn't he?" said Ben.

Neither of the other two spoke for a moment then, to change the subject, Ravi asked,

"Fancy a game of pool Ben?"

"I play the winner," said Juan.

They walked through into the rest room and Juan sat and watched as Ben and Ravi began to play.

~~~~~~~~~~~~~

In the photocopying room was a large printer, capable of many different types of copy or form. Rick was comparing the colour of a ticket to the A4 pink sheet he had on the desk.

"It's only the same colour," he said enthusiastically to Stuart. "I mean, this isn't even going to be difficult." With this, Rick and Stuart started laughing.

"Leave you to it," said Stuart and he walked out of the kitchen and back into the computer room.

Rick printed out about 100 tickets, hurriedly put them in his bag and went back to his real work.

Half an hour later Rick went to his locker, opened the door and stooped down to the bottom shelf. Two bottles clanked against what sounded like a sea of glass. He picked them up and put them under his jacket and went off to the security office. When he entered, Ivan had his feet on his desk and a reasonably warmish glow on his face. When he saw Rick his eyes lit up.

"That beer's blooming marvellous," he said.

"Good, I brought you two more," said Rick.

Ivan could almost have kissed him but felt guilty and said,

"I can't take all your beer like this." He glanced at the bottles and resisted the urge to lick his lips.

"I made ten gallons," Rick said, "Two little bottles won't hurt. Go on, get it down yer neck, Ivan," Ivan smiled.

"Thanks. I wish all them other lads were like you. I'm really enjoying this beer."

"I might drop some more round later. If you don't drink it here you could take it home with you," said the almost saintly Rick.

Ivan wondered why he was getting pampered like this, but was grateful and could only reply,

"OK great. Thanks Rick."

Having done his good deed for the day our hero returned to the computer room with a small grin on his face.

It was now 2.15 and Eugene's car came down the road at breakneck speed. Inside, Eugene was crouching, head half under the steering wheel: hand groping near the foot pedals. He suddenly sat up, then screeched to a halt next to the security gates.

Ivan, thinking all sorts of things could be going on, ran outside, only to see Eugene's car. He walked round to the driver's side and saw Eugene ripping a plastic bag from around his accelerator pedal. Putting a jar of coffee and box of tea bags on the passenger seat, Eugene then picked up two pints of milk from the passenger's footwell. Ivan, felt happier, but wanted to ask the inevitable,

"Everything OK?"

Eugene looked up and said,

"It was until that stupid cat ran across the road. I braked and this lot fell around the pedals and wedged between my feet and the accelerator. I'll be all right now though,"

Eugene said confidently. Ivan just nodded his head, thinking,

"If only that were true."

At three o'clock Stuart went round to each member of the shift and told them to meet in the rest room. About five minutes later, as they were all sitting around the pool table Stuart handed out some photocopies. The paper they now held contained a long memo signed at the bottom by Ralph Parkett, the department manager. The lads knew him as Captain Sensible. He smoked small cigars, worked longer than his designated eight hours and was a typical administrator. To look at him you would only think of him as middle management.

Everything in Ralph's office was colour-coded, even the telephones. He had devised forms for everything: from stains on the floors to the number of paper cups in the kitchen. He lived and breathed his work. Nothing was too much trouble. One of the senior managers had only to suggest something and he would do it, but do it with almost military precision.

Once a year he arranged an outing for all employees of the firm. This made him feel like a vital cog in the large wheel. The previous month he had asked all the managers within AMO if there was anyone interested in their respective departments who would like to attend this year's event.

"Everyone read it?" asked Stuart lethargically.

"I see Captain Sensible's going in for his knighthood again," said Jeff.

"This could be a laugh," said Rick with a smile almost the width of the rest room.

The memo confirmed that Ralph would be booking them onto a privately chartered train to Lincoln where there would be something for everyone to do. The train would have a bar on board and travel directly to Lincoln after it left London. Ralph had suggested various things available to visit like art galleries, a funfair, a hologram exhibition and a jazz club, open from noon onwards.

Although they called him Captain Sensible, the lads knew he would try and include something in the outing that would interest all of them. Totally out of character, aware of the potential risks involved, he had included the news that there would be a brewery tour in Lincoln and, on the way back, a beer festival in Collingham, a small town back down the railway line. Ralph had sent a letter requesting more information. Stuart and Rick knew this already because, the night before, they had opened his purple drawer. Purple was his miscellaneous drawer and it contained information about outings, amongst other things.

The manager of the brewery, Mr Forbes-Blanchard had written back thanking him for his inquiry. He said he would have no trouble in accommodating up to 200 visitors on the day in question. Included in his letter were two pink tickets inscribed with *Free beer with this voucher* and he implied he would send two vouchers for each person when the tour was confirmed. Cunningly, Rick had forged 100 of these earlier so the lads would each get a few more free beers.

Ralph's memo ended with a request that he be informed of final numbers by the middle of the following week so he could finalise the details of the trip with the railway company and the brewery.

Stuart produced his own sheet of paper and held it up.

"This is a memo to all of you from me and Rick," he said excitedly.

Then, as everyone in the room was looking at him, he screwed the piece of paper up and put it in his pocket.

"Keep this in your heads, this could be the biggest laugh we have ever had." Stuart went on,

"Nine o'clock train bar opens, twelve o'clock brewery visit, three o'clock beer festival. Show of hands please."

Immediately, all the hands went up with a cheer, except Dennis's. He was tapping at his calculator and frowning.

"What about the overtime I'll miss?" he asked.

Loud comments were shouted out,

"Miser."

"Skinflint."

"Tightwad."

Stuart waited for the noise to die down and said,

"If you miss this you will be kicking yourself," again, he paused, "I've got things planned for this you wouldn't believe."

"Oh yeah, like what?" Dennis asked.

"Like forged beer vouchers for a start. Show him Rick."

Rick pulled out a wad of vouchers from his pocket and passed them round.

"This is the original," said Stuart, showing it round. He was greeted with enthusiastic voices.

"Brilliant." said Bruce.

"Nice one," said Charlie.

"Oh go on then, count me in," said Dennis regretfully.

"So far, eight of the day shift and six of the evening shift want to go, plus a few uninvited guests."

As Stuart said this, laughter rang out. There were several disreputable characters the lads invited each year to pep up proceedings. Needless to say, Ralph would ban them from coming but they would turn up each year under a new name and in a slight disguise. A unanimous decision was made by the shift: they were all going on the Lincoln trip.

Stuart insisted everyone would go fully equipped with their own rambling bag. This was open to the owner's interpretation but usually consisted of a combination of avalanche foam, smoke bombs, potato guns, silly string, rocket balloons, fart spray, fake blood, trick knives, exploding cigars, and home-made flour bombs. These bags would be made up the week before and added to as required. In addition to this, backup plastic bags of larger items would also go on the trip. These included joke shop staples such as false bottoms, bald heads, wigs, hats and even a pair of false breasts. Experience over the years had found that some items were used more than others, but by the time of the outing, the choice of equipment would be at full capacity.

Chapter 3

Toby Fanshaw's Dial-Up

After ten minutes the rest room was clear and everyone was back at their work places. In view of the desperate food situation they were forced to attend the restaurant. The restaurant block was about five minutes away. The night shift only went there when the need was dire. Knowing no one had any choice, Stuart had gone round to see who wanted to go.

At 4.05 Stuart, Dennis, Rick, Tim, Bruce, Charlie and Jeff arrived at the restaurant block. They were all looking apprehensive, some crossing their fingers, some crossing themselves religiously.

"I wonder where Ivan is?" asked Tim trying to take his mind off the ensuing culinary shock.

"Enjoying my beer," replied Rick. On the way through he had left another two bottles for Ivan.

"He'll be legless by 6.00," Rick laughed as he said this and the others all joined in with him.

Two black double doors faced them as they reached the top of the stairs on the second floor of the building. The smell of what used to be food lingered with the awful stench of stale air fresheners.

As they walked through the doors, six fairly large AMO company lorry drivers sat looking pale but fed. The plates in front of them containing what looked like the remains of failed biology experiments.

A notice on the left side of the counter said *Menu*. Someone had crossed out *Menu* and replaced it with *Reading this may damage your health.*

The order for the brave, magnificent seven was minute steak and chips four times, chop and chips twice and full breakfast for Dennis. This order was relayed by Stuart shouting to a space at the back of the counter where heat and foul smells were emanating. As they sat down to wait for what could be their last meal, the space where the smells were coming from enquired in a loud deep voice,

"Is that double portions?" A resounding,

"No, single," was the quick reply.

After about ten minutes a large white wobbling mass put four plates on the top of the counter and shouted,

"Four steaks."

No sooner had these been collected than three more plates were thrust down. The meals were free to staff on night shift, but even so, not many entered the restaurant.

Looking down at his plate Charlie said,

"Man this minute steak looks like it's been cooking for about a month."

"My chop's been panel beaten," said Bruce.

"I reckon I might see all of this again later," shuddered Jeff.

The lads, trying not to taste the substances, quickly emptied the seven plates of their contents, all except for the bits which could not be identified. Various comments were made about insurance policies and private health care in case of food poisoning, but at least they were still alive – just.

On leaving the restaurant it was discussed whether or not to send get well soon cards to the six lorry drivers who ate there every night. It was decided best not, as their taste buds were already depleted and they must by now have zinc-lined stomachs.

The night was beginning to drag a bit, but the sight of Ivan, now quite red-faced, greeted them at the entrance as they returned to the computer block.

"Hello lads," he said loudly as they passed him. Rick made sure he was the last one to go by, hoping for a chance to see how Ivan really was.

"Blooming marvellous that beer of yours," Ivan said with a thumbs up sign.

Rick glanced behind Ivan's desk to where he had put the last two bottles. They had not yet been consumed. These were special ones. They were double strength barley wine from last year. Rick knew by the time Ivan got to them he wouldn't care what he was drinking and the reason for his generosity could be revealed.

By five o'clock all of the night shift had eaten and it was now just a matter of whiling away the few remaining hours. The main and urgent work had been completed and all the vital print-outs and tapes were in the relevant areas to await collection by van later. Just a few small things to do in the usual routine way until the day shift arrived.

Rick had volunteered to sit at the main console, checking if anything needed doing. His bag at the side of his chair containing four bottles of homebrew to keep him company. He knew if, in the unlikely event that Ivan came through, he could stop him from going to the rest room. This was a ploy he had tried successfully before.

Tim had devised an end of shift game called Flour Roulette. Six, smallish parcels were made up and passed round as the shift sat in a circle. The person who had the small parcel hit the person on their right over the head with it and so on. When a complete circuit had been done everyone was then blindfolded. At Tim's discretion a parcel containing flour was introduced. After ten minutes of this, the rest room looked like a scene from the Snowman. Anyone left without any flour on them helped Tim to clear up. That was, when they had all stopped laughing.

Thoughtfully, Stuart suggested that next they play 'Toby Fanshaw's Dial-Up'. This was a name Rick had chosen from a local phone book one night shift, while blindfolded and fairly drunk.

From an international phone book Stuart had obtained the numbers for various countries. After a bit of dialling he got through to Mr Larry Weiss from Dayton, Ohio. The following conversation ensued:

"Hello. This is Toby Fanshaw's Dial-Up line from London, England. To whom am I speaking this fine day?" spoken in a very upper class English accent.

"This is Larry Weiss, but it's the middle of the night."

Stuart cut in, "How would you like to win two weeks' paid holiday, with £1,000 spending money in Windsor Castle?"

"Will the Queen be there?" asked Larry.

"All of the Royal family. You'll even meet the corgis. How about it Larry?"

"Yeah sure, what do I need to do?" asked Larry more interested now.

"OK Larry, where are you from? Think now, old boy."

"Dayton, Ohio," answered Larry.

"That's right. You've won the holiday. Congratulations." said Stuart.

A large cheer went up at the other end of Stuart's phone and Larry was heard shouting to his family,

"We're going to see the Queen of England."

As the commotion was died down Charlie took the phone. He was Stuart's partner in this game, although Larry didn't know this.

"Hello. Hello, Mr Weiss?" Charlie said in a strong American accent.

"Yeah, who are you?" asked Larry.

"I'm Special Agent Columbo, New York FBI. This call has been intercepted. For reasons of national security do not speak again. Goodnight sir."

As Charlie put the phone down the whole room erupted with laughter and thoughts of poor old Larry from Ohio.

It was now getting fairly light outside as Jeff and Bruce were ringing Mr Muller from Frankfurt, Germany. There would be a few more lucky winners from France, Italy and Belgium. As usual, part of this game was if the person could not speak English, they had to go and wake up someone who could. Stuart had the relevant information written in all the languages they phoned.

Rick had not done anything but drink his beer for the last half hour and was getting a bit restless. As it was so quiet, he thought he'd take a wander over to Ivan's security hut. As he reached the front window, he quietly looked in. He was faced with a balding head lolling back and forth and loud snoring noises. Turning the door handle gently, he eased his way in.

Ivan had now consumed the last two, very strong bottles of home brew.

Looking down into the small washing bag he had brought with him, Rick took a small amount of shaving foam and put it over Ivan's right eyebrow. Gently, he shaved off the eyebrow. In fact, Ivan was so inebriated, Rick was able to remove all excess hair without Ivan being the least bit aware. Obligingly, Ivan lolled forward presenting his balding head to Rick. In an instant, an indelible felt tip had written 'Balls to AMO' across the top of the head.

It only remained for Rick to blow-up the plastic doll they had all chipped in for at last year's outing. He turned Ivan round on his swivel chair and put his back to the door. The blow-up doll was placed on Ivan's lap. Rick made for the door but then stopped. Out came the video camera he had borrowed from Charlie. After taking a few shots he made his way back to the work station.

It was now six o'clock and the last round of Toby Fanshaw's Dial-Up had been played. A triumphant Dennis and Juan had won with their call to Señor Lopez in Madrid. All had been going well when Juan cut in with fluent Spanish as Pepe Heraldez, Chief of Police for Madrid. He told Señor Lopez that he would consider him for further investigation and not to attend any bullfights for a year.

As he slammed down the phone the rest of the shift needed to know what Juan had said. Juan replied,

"He try to bribe me but I tell him not to shut de stable door after de horse, he has farted."

On hearing this the lads decided this was the winning call.

"Speech, speech," they all cried, as was customary for the winner of this game.

"My Inglees is not great, but my Spanish Magnífico. Bravo, Dennis and Juan de champions." he said, jubilantly.

A loud cheer greeted these words. From outside the room came a shout.

"Shut up." It was Rick, coming to tell of his exploits further afield.

"Quick, come and have a look at this," he said, hurriedly.

They all marched along to Ivan's hut and peeped through the window. Ivan's position was basically the same as when Rick had left him, except he was not cuddling the blow-up doll quite so tightly. Amid the snores and smell of beer they took it in turns to inspect Ivan and his partner. Then they walked away, sniggering and holding their hands to their faces to keep as quiet as they could. Once back inside the computer building Rick turned to the laughing rabble and said,

"That'll teach him."

"What for?" asked Ravi, inquiringly.

"Well, three weeks ago he reported me for drinking on the day shift after the bar had shut," Rick continued, "What's the point of having a bar in the building if you can't enjoy it?"

More laughter followed.

"Shall I make the tea?" asked Eugene.

"Yeah, but be careful," said Stuart.

Eugene went off to make the last brew of the night shift. This shift had been quite an eventful one, even for their standards.

Everything seemed to be quiet, especially Ivan, but he was due a surprise visit. Someone with a liking for home brew and revenge had rung the Security Controller, Mr Doug Cheltan. This man was in charge of all AMO security and had to investigate the sighting of a herd of cows in Sulcrem House car park.

When he had arrived at the building he had burst into the security hut expecting to find a record of Ivan's log of the night's events. Instead, the sight that befell him made him step back in amazement.

"Ivan. Ivan," he shouted.

Nothing happened. Ivan didn't move. Mr Cheltan turned Ivan's chair around and in doing so the blow-up doll slipped from Ivan's grasp and slid to the floor. The words 'Balls to AMO' became visible to Mr Cheltan. He leaned forward to shake Ivan awake when he noticed Ivan's face looked different. Remembering the cows, he quickly shook Ivan who woke with a start.

"What's the meaning of this and where are the cows?" Doug asked angrily.

Ivan just looked dazed and confused.

"Oh come on man, speak," Cheltan paused.

No sound came from Ivan, still confused with eyes rolling.

"Right, I'll sort these cows out first then I'll be back."

With this, the Security Controller stepped backwards on the doll. A loud exhalation of air made Ivan jump.

He mumbled, "That beer's ruined me."

Wondering how the plastic object had got there Ivan began to try to make sense of what was going on.

"Cows? What cows?" he thought.

25

He pushed the doll under his desk and hid it with his jacket, then staggered out to the car park.

Mr Cheltan had discovered nothing. He had searched the whole perimeter of the building and could find no trace of the cattle. It had puzzled him why anyone should want to move cows in a big town that was miles from any farm, let alone do it at night. However, as it was now early morning and the time of day farmers would be about, he thought it was right to investigate.

A figure lurched towards him, strange lettering on his head, red eyes, and one eyebrow. Was this the beast, the evil one?

"Wha tha cows?" said Ivan, his speech functioning as poorly as his legs.

"There are no cows. Now go and get some black coffee. I'll arrange to have you taken home," said Mr Cheltan.

"Ry ho," a puzzled Ivan mumbled as he went into the computer building.

"You've not heard the last of this," Mr Cheltan shouted after him.

Meanwhile, most of the shift were in the rest room crouching down by the windows watching, tea mugs in hand. As Ivan made his way slowly to the kitchen a loud cheer went up. Ivan said nothing and tacked slowly onward like an old yacht in a gale. At last he made it to the kettle, but as he looked down saw four cups of black coffee, each with his name on. He reached for the first one, feeling a bit better about the shift as they had kindly made him these drinks. He was just about to take the first sip when he stopped and poured it down the sink. He held the empty cup up. Everyone looked in his direction.

"You won't get me with your laxative tea," he drawled.

While Ivan negotiated his way back to the kettle a chorus rang out.

"You won't get me with your laxative tea. You won't get me with your laxative tea," then more laughter from the rest room.

Outside, a squeaking black and rust-coloured moped made its way to the security hut. Sitting astride the saddle was a thin, six foot, thirty year old male with long hair and a beard. It was Jack, the morning cleaner. Due to his appearance and outlook on life most of the shifts addressed him as "Oy, hippy."

Jack was well liked because of his easy-going nature and passive stance. He agreed with everyone. It was the best way he thought.

After parking his bike by the side of the security hut he walked through and looked at Ivan's chair and who was sitting in it.

"Pass please?" commanded Doug Cheltan, obviously annoyed to be at Sulcrem House.

"Oh yeah, hang on man, it's right here. Sorry man," said Jack, obligingly.

Looking at the photopass Cheltan said,

"I'll be remembering you mate. Go on, in you go."

"Thanks man, very kind man," Jack said, nodding as if he had just left royalty.

He casually wandered to the cleaning room. On various occasions he had been given the odd £5 and £10 notes from members of this shift for the mess that had been made. He appreciated the way they had always tried to clear up after themselves though.

As Jack was sorting out his buckets etc, he heard a loud angry shout from the toilet block. Jack went over to investigate. There, staring into the large mirror was Ivan who had just discovered he was an eyebrow amputee and his head had become a notice board.

Innocently, Jack walked in saying,

"Hi man, it's a great day yeah?"

Ivan turned to him and started to shake and go red in the face. Jack made for the door but could still hear Ivan shouting obscenities, even when he was right at the far end of the corridor.

Chapter 4

Sally's Here

A fairly robust AMO security man in a van had arrived to take Ivan home. He had been briefed on the situation by Doug Cheltan and allowed Ivan to make a few disdainful remarks at the shift as he left. It was now 6.30, only half an hour to go till the day shift would begin.

Even though the night shift had been an eventful one, the sight of an all-male staff for nearly eight hours had begun to wear thin. That's why everyone eagerly awaited the arrival of Sally, the receptionist. She was five feet one, slimly built, attractive and always dressed to please. At twenty-six she had collected a long line of boyfriends but they were all put off by her hobby of onion pickling.

After a night out with her, the various admirers thought their luck was in when they got back to her place. The lights would be dimmed, a video put on and she would suggest sitting on the sofa. Then, bingo, out would come a jar of onions. It was a ritual she had and one she never broke for anyone. Several of the lads had been round for the night of their lives only to play second fiddle to a pickled onion.

One tragic night Bruce had been to the local joke and fancy dress shop and tried knocking on Sally's door dressed as an onion. The poor bloke had been hoping she would drag him in and start peeling him. No such luck. She did admire his spirit though, and offered to go to the pub with him.

She was known as the onion junkie at AMO. They all thought it was a tragedy. All except Jack who said it was great to express your real feelings and emotions and Sally loves pickling and eating onions,

"That's great, man."

Whatever her habits at home that did not matter after she arrived at work. There, she leaned and stretched all over the place, taking this and that to and fro with the full approval of all whose eyes she brightened. One particular shift she had come in wearing a short black miniskirt and was about to say goodbye to Stuart as he left when he said,

"You've made an old man very happy."

In the middle of the building Jeff was on the second floor looking at his watch and then out of the window up to the top of the road. At 6.45 Sally turned the corner and started to walk towards the building. Jeff immediately picked up the phone on the desk beside him and rang down to Stuart,

"Sally's here," he said excitedly.

Stuart informed most of the shift and everyone found a job around reception. Some checked baskets of work, others pretended to be studying computer printouts, but all were waiting for Sally. As she walked through the doors of reception everyone pretended to be busy.

"Morning all," she said.

"Morning," came the mass reply, everyone still really busy.

Then, as she turned her back to take off her coat, all eyes were upon her. Whatever she did for the next few minutes had the maximum audience. A real perk of the job was to end the night shift with Sally.

The clock in reception showed 6.50 when, in walked Keith, the day shift leader. He had been at AMO longer than anyone on shift. He would rather be gardening than surrounded by air conditioning and the hum of a computer room. He did his job well but, whenever possible, drank large amounts of scotch to deaden the pain of his indoor existence.

"Morning Sally."

"Morning Keith," Sally replied.

Keith put his briefcase on the office table and went to the kitchen for coffee.

A few minutes later a muscular, short-haired young man came through the doors carrying a car magazine.

"Hello Inglees pig, Barry," said a loud Juan.

"Hello, filthy Spanish type," replied his friend.

They pretended to fight and tussle, but they were good friends.

Several more of the day shift were now arriving and it was time to hand over the night's work, or what was left of it. Despite all the mucking about, the work always got done and it had been known for night shift workers to stay on and help the day shift for a while if they were short-staffed.

Stuart reminded Keith to get as many more to the work's outing as possible. Keith agreed and then said goodbye to the trickling line of bodies leaving the building.

In the car park Stuart said, "Back to mine for a beer if you want."

A few days before each of the previous three Friday night shifts Stuart had ordered a barrel of bitter. All the lads had chipped in and they had three or four pints before getting into the sleeping bags they had brought with them. The first pint usually went down fast, the second a little slower and the next two at a reasonable pace.

Apart from various milk floats out on their morning rounds, it was still fairly quiet for a Saturday morning. Most of the cars going back to Stuart's had their windows open to keep the drivers more alert. On arriving at Stuart's, shady figures, awkwardly carrying sleeping bags, waddled into his living room. When they were all ready Stuart pointed to various areas,

"Glasses, barrel, fish tank - fish tank not toilet – toilet upstairs. Right boys, tuck in."

Rick was the first to pour himself a pint, just as on the previous occasions. He didn't drive so he tended to drink a lot. The ones with cars would have a good sleep at Stuart's and then walk up to the local pub for a meal and another pint. Stuart's neighbours were used to seeing cars around most of the weekends after night shifts.

When they had first started going back to Stuart's house there were only a few of them and they just had some cans of beer, but as the numbers had grown it was a barrel of best bitter that was needed. As most of the guys were single they could do as they pleased, and usually did. They all had girlfriends but were at varying stages of commitment and the girls were kept from knowing most of what went on.

Stuart's girlfriend was working away in Saudi on a nursing contract. Conveniently, the boys had worked out that if they were at Stuart's all weekend their girlfriends would not know where they were. One weekend in the month could be a total drink-up with no hassles. For the next three months, until Stuart's girlfriend returned, that's what they intended to do.

"A toast, a toast," Rick shouted and silence fell on the room. "To Ivan and his eyebrow."

"To Ivan," came the reply and laughter rang out once more.

Then Jeff stood up. "A toast, a toast," again, silence. "To beer," he said.

"Beer," came the reply.

During the next couple of hours various stories and jokes were swapped. Some were about Eugene who, like Juan and Ravi were not at Stuart's house, but the eight who were, just relaxed and enjoyed each other's company. By 9.30 only Rick was still awake, drinking happily.

The next seven hours passed peacefully with various trips to Stuart's toilet and Rick pouring a half pint of beer each time he passed the barrel to take with him on the journey. Suddenly, an exhaust backfired from next door's drive and woke everyone with a start. Mr Myford, Stuart's next-door neighbour, had kick-started his motorbike and sidecar. He tried to save money whenever possible and always pushed his motorbike in and out of the garage to do just that.

On Wednesdays and Sundays mornings he practised his trombone, which he played for the Salvation Army. Stuart called him by his first name, Ernie, and was glad to have such a tolerant neighbour.

Over the course of the next half hour a slow procession of washing and freshening up began. Again, Rick had been first and was sitting on the sofa with a pint and a cigarette. As six o'clock approached they were all ready and left for the local pub, *The Tardis*. It was named in honour of the 'Dr Who' programme and despite its small facade, seemed a lot bigger inside.

The landlord of the freehouse was Neil. His wife, Carol, did the food. Coming from a lively Birmingham pub the couple had fallen in love with the *Flying Eagle* but knew they needed to make a few changes. They had the turnover but it needed re-vamping, so Neil had suggested they call the pub *The Tardis* and Carol proposed they offer proper hot meals instead of snacks. Right from their first month it had done well and now, a year on, it was thriving.

"Eight pints of stout and -" before Stuart could say any more Neil said,

"Six dozen oysters, right?"

A small cheer went up and on hearing this, Carol appeared saying,

"Look out, it's the Mafia." She then asked "Are you lot hungry?"

Tim approached the bar with his jacket hanging around his shoulders. He put a serviette at each corner of his mouth and said to Carol,

"You fixa us a da biga meal or we fixa da Tardis, understand?"

"Leave it with me Mr Brando," Carol replied and went off to cook for the Sicilian octet.

33

Everyone stayed around the bar chatting to Neil who knew the boys liked a drink and a laugh but never caused any trouble in his pub. He did have a few unsavoury characters who frequented the pub from time to time, but generally, there was a good, happy atmosphere.

Only one other person was in the pub: an old man with his cap and raincoat on, a half pint in front of him. All around were pictures of various 'Dr Who' scenes. There was a dalek at one end of the pub and a cyberman at the other. The theme music from the cult TV programme played at Neil's discretion.

At about eight o'clock it started to get busy and extra bar staff arrived to help out. Being a hard working couple in their forties, Neil and Carol never minded a few regulars having a drink after hours at the weekend. Needless to say, the eight shift workers from AMO were usually amongst them. On occasions, other staff members from AMO joined the merry band. Neil had a karaoke machine and encouraged anyone to sing along to the record, with words displayed on the TV screen above the bar.

Everyone, except Rick, tried to drink at a slower pace than normal until at least 9.30 when the singing started in the almost full pub.

Neil picked up the microphone and announced the fun was about to start. The first song was to be sung by Neil and Carol. They did a version of Sonny & Cher's 'I Got You Babe' from the sixties. Neil wore what looked like half a sheep in a waistcoat and Carol wore a long, dark-haired wig and a miniskirt. Showing no fear, they belted out the song and got a loud cheer when they had finished. Various combinations of songs were then tried by several alcoholically challenged members of the pub and, by 10.15, the atmosphere was electric.

As the boys from AMO began to succumb to the wonders of malt and hops Charlie decided it was their turn to sing. He handed Neil a video and asked,

"Can you get this on the screen for us when you're ready?"

"It's not a rude film is it?" queried Neil.

"No, but you put it on, we'll sing, ok?"

A short while later, Neil waved his arm to where the lads were sitting to let them know it was their turn. Picking up the microphone he said,

"And now I've no idea what to expect from this lot but, take it away the AMO Singers."

As the video started up, eight red-eyed, laughing, merry inebriates stood up and brushed back their hair and curled their lips. Attempts at waving one leg to the side were tried, but it led to slight overbalancing. The pub crowd giggled at the sight before them.

Suddenly, the screen was filled with a view of the AMO building. The scene then changed to a large office window over the top of which, in large letters, was a sign saying *Boss's Office*. Outside the window was a motorbike on which sat the blow-up doll Ivan had met the previous night. As the camera zoomed in on the doll, a hand, holding a microphone, moved to her mouth. From inside the pub eight songsheets were produced for eight Elvis impersonators singing '(Let Me Be Your) Teddy Bear'. A laughing audience joined in.

The next scene on the tape was an empty mailroom and the doll with a large ticket around her arm. With the camera closing in once more, the ticket read 'Return to Sender'. The Elvis impersonators started singing in unison again. Half way through the song, a hand with an eye dropper, made the doll cry. The screen then showed a shot of the mailman, Duncan, puzzling over the unusual package, unaware of the camera.

As the song came to an end the scene changed to a car park in which stood a green sports car with smoke coming from the exhaust. Brian from the day shift was seen swearing and then, enter Ivan, our hero, giving the car a push. Not even a day old, this film showed the activities of the previous evening. As Brian skidded towards the video camera the lads in the pub sang 'All Shook Up' and nearly everyone in the pub joined in.

Before the song ended, the next scene appeared. It had been edited in by Charlie at Stuart's house a few hours earlier.

The start this time was Eugene. Sellotaped to a lamp post and gagged. He was struggling until cool black liquid was poured over him. This had happened a few months ago after he had spilled hot chocolate on the pool table. 'King Creole' was the tune being played but this version was called 'King Creosote'. During the video a large black arm with a soup ladle could be seen pouring more of the black cold coffee mixed with stout over Eugene.

And so, another good night was enjoyed by everyone at *The Tardis*. After a few nightcaps, everyone went back to Stuart's to make sure the barrel of bitter wasn't feeling too lonely.

On the way, hunger set in once more. Dennis led the procession down the high road to the kebab house. During the next half hour, warm meat, bread and salad were cast into the lake of bitter, near belly button creek.

Once at Stuart's, after the obligatory toilet break, everyone sat down to watch the edition of *Match of the Day* that had been recorded earlier. Rick handed everyone a beer and then volunteered to sit by the barrel as all the seats were taken. It was a hardship he felt only he could endure.

As sixteen, half-closing eyes watched the first game Bruce asked,

"Everyone going to the match tomorrow morning?"

"Who're we playing?" asked Jeff.

"Blundon Transport 3rd Team," Dennis pitched in.

"They'll be in a worse state than we will," said Tim with a giggle.

As the television recording finished, it didn't take long before seven of the lads were fast asleep. Rick polished off all the beer from the stray glasses and then had a quick half pint from the barrel before attempting to get into his sleeping bag.

Now all that remained was to hope they would all wake in time for the weekly match in the local Sunday league.

Chapter 5

The Big Match

It was 9.15 and the captain of the AMO team, Ralph Parkett, was inspecting his boots. He breathed on them, then gave them a buff up with a cloth, then placed them neatly in his sports bag with the rest of his immaculate kit. He picked up a piece of A4 size paper and drew tactical patterns on it: frowning, studying, surveying. This carried on for fifteen minutes until he had several sheets.

When he had decided, on Jeff's advice, to form a football team, naturally the captaincy had had to be his.

Meanwhile, back at Stuart's house, no-one stirred. It could have been a scene from the Seven Dwarves, but who was Snow White? Next door, Stuart's neighbour, Ernie, began to limber up a beautiful shiny trombone using his musical talents. A few practice notes then straight into 'Onward, Christian Soldiers'. The fact he was in his living room made it easier for the sound to carry through to Stuart's house next door.

Inside his sleeping bag Jeff stirred, different musical notes hitting his ears. He dreamed the lads had gone to a jazz concert but somehow there was an invasion by the Salvation Army and they took over the stage. Unable to move he felt he was being taken over by a strange power. More and more notes pounded in his ears until: knock, knock, a large metallic thumping. Was it machine gun fire?

Jeff's eyes opened wide and then half shut again. A louder knock knock and he realised there was someone at the front door. Getting slowly out of his sleeping bag he shuffled to the door to let in a fairly fresh-faced Eugene. Never thinking he would be pleased to see Eugene, Jeff said happily,

"Hello Mate." Eugene replied with, "All right Jeff?"

They walked back into the front room which, considering the amount of beer that had been consumed the night before, was fairly clean and tidy. Kicking at the sides of the sleeping bags, Eugene and Jeff woke up Charlie, Bruce, Rick, Tim and Ben. Glad to be alive and awake they thanked their two colleagues with a stream of obscenities. This was a complete contrast to the scene next door where Ernie was really getting into his playing now. Rick shook his head, went to the stereo and put on the radio. He then walked through to the kitchen and switched on the kettle.

"What time's kick off, Jeff?" inquired Bruce.

"Eleven o'clock. We've got about an hour, better wake Stuart."

Jeff picked up an old newspaper, pulled out a page and tore it in half. Quietly, creeping up the stairs and opening Stuart's door, he crept over to the bedside table and picked up the cigarettes and lighter that had been placed there the previous evening. Returning to the landing, he stood under the smoke alarm just outside Stuart's bedroom. The rest of the lads gathered at the bottom of the stairs to watch Jeff as he lit the newspaper and waited. Seconds later a piercing siren started up, he let the paper burn for as long as possible then blew it out and headed down the stairs.

Thinking the worst, Stuart bolted out of bed and on to the landing, only to collide with a startled Dennis who had been sleeping in the bed in the next room. As Dennis was about ten stone heavier than Stuart, the collision pushed Stuart three feet into the bathroom. He landed with a thump and, as he did so, a loud cheer went up from the group at the foot of the stairs.

"Morning Stuart," said a giggling Eugene.

"Shut up," came the morose reply.

As Rick passed around tea and coffee to everyone Stuart started making endless rounds of toast. This was interrupted by Ben commenting,

"You two make a lovely couple."

"Thanks dear," replied Rick.

The following half hour saw a remarkable change in everyone and by the time the second round of hot drinks had been served the lads were almost raring to go. At 10.30 they left for the ground which was only a ten minute drive away.

They had played Blundon Transport III away earlier in the season and won 1-2. After the game they had found a very hospitable lounge where the beer had flowed freely. Both teams, being near the top of the twelve-strong league, had a strong respect for each other. However, both teams had a healthier respect for a good drink up the night after a game.

At Endis Recreation Ground, Ralph, the team captain, paced to and fro checking and re-checking his watch. Of course, he always got to the ground about half an hour before anyone else. A shiny black sports car approached. It was Norman, Barry and Juan. The groundsman had just opened the dressing rooms as Ravi walked through the gates. Now inside the dressing room, Ralph placed all the football shirts on pegs in number order, he then sat down and got out the tactical papers he had written earlier. When the other four were sitting by their shirts he handed out a sheet to each of them.

Outside in the car park the rest of the team were arriving and a noisy procession moved forward to the dressing room to change for battle. After exchanging greetings with their fellow gladiators, they sat looking puzzled at Ralph's diagrams.

Ralph began,

"Team today: Charlie in goal, full backs Eugene and Jeff, centre backs Bruce and Ravi, midfield Juan, myself and Norman, up front Barry, Ben and Tim, subs Dennis and Stuart."

Being the size he was Dennis was only brought on if the other team played dirty. Not many escaped his wrath if they had hurt his teammates.

Stuart did not really want to play because, at forty-two, he felt his playing days were over, but he always turned up.

Ralph continued, "We will play a 4-3-3 formation and if you look at my tactical plan-"

"What, dis thing? It looks like a printout from air traffic control at Madrid Airport," interrupted Juan.

"No, it's the new Highway Code," said Eugene, trying to impress.

Before Ralph had a chance to continue, an increasing volume of noise could be heard approaching. As the noise reached its loudest level, the opposition entered the dressing room.

Not many pleasantries would be exchanged before the game as both teams wanted to win the match. After the game though, would be quite different. This was Sunday football, after all, and drinking and socialising were all part of it.

As both teams left the dressing room, the rapid tapping of nylon studs on the concrete floor outside could be heard, which slowly faded as they made contact with the grass on the side of the pitch.

Footballs flew around in both goals as the two teams gingerly warmed up prior to kick off. A sprinkling of people looked on, spread out along the sidelines of the pitch. These games were never well attended.

From a separate part of the ground the referee approached, running on to the grass and checking his watch simultaneously. He blew his whistle and shouted,

"Captains please," whilst searching for his notebook in his only top pocket.

Ralph, jogging up thoughtfully, shook the referee's hand, then the opposing captain won the toss for once and chose to defend the goal they were currently in.

Something looked odd to Ralph on the left wing but as the sun was strong and they were about to kick off he ignored it.

Various shouts of encouragement came from both teams such as "Bar's open soon lads" and, "It's the Ref's round first." Smiling cautiously the match official blew his whistle to start the game.

Ben passed to Barry, who played it back to Juan, the team advanced forward. Juan chipped a long ball to the far post – Ralph thought, "Great move, I must include it in my tactics. Now come on, score."

The ball hung in the air but who was this going for it? A player with hair half way down his back. "Who is that?" thought Ralph.

The mystery player rose, attacked the ball by heading it to the right hand side of the goal. A large, hairy black object flew towards the goalkeeper, with the ball going in off the other post. The goalkeeper squealed. Ralph's team mates cheered, "Goal." and Tim went to the goalie and asked for his wig back. This provoked a slight altercation between them. The referee intervened and warned Tim,

"Any more nonsense and you will be off."

Blundon Transport III adopted a more physical approach to the game after that. After they had scored the equaliser and injured Norman, it was time for the ultimate deterrent Ralph decided.

"Warm up Dennis." he shouted.

Dennis considered that, at twenty stone, taking off his tent-like tracksuit was all the warm-up he needed. When the referee called him on to the field, the opposition went a bit quiet, acknowledging the mass they were about to face up to.

Strangely, the game got fairly tame after that. Dennis only had to look at a rival player on the ball and they passed it straight away. One brave defender did venture near Dennis but ended up two yards down the pitch on contact.

As the referee blew his whistle for half time, the score stood at 1-1. Ralph used the few minutes to ask his team why they were not using the tactics he had shown them and to reprimand Tim for the wig incident.

Dennis was pushed up front for the second half and Sulcrem Utd finished up winning 4-1. Blundon Transport III's defenders looked shell-shocked due to the attack by the twenty stone mountain. Despite this, the two teams shook hands, knowing battle was done and the fun could begin again.

Stuart, the unused substitute, had been busy during the match. He had indulged in a spot of dressing room sabotage. The players retired to find different footwear to the ones they had arrived in: one odd shoe and one odd sock. As things were swapped back to normal, all in good humour, Ralph gave directions for getting to the Sulcrem House Bar to the losers. Blundon Transport III had arrived by minibus and the teetotal driver looked apprehensive as they boarded the vehicle ready for some refreshment down the road.

By one o'clock the bar was pleasantly filled with the two teams and a few of the overtime shift. Two large trays of shandy were quickly downed followed by several lager and lemonade tops. A tray of sandwiches went round, then another and by 2.30 the atmosphere was lively, but controlled.

On his fourth large scotch, Keith, today's overtime shift leader, sat where he had been since the bar opened. Alongside him were two computer engineers waiting for a problem to fix with their computer toolkits and specialist knowledge. Keith, between swift swigs of his drink, was explaining the need for Latin names for plants and the delights of an herbaceous border. One of the engineers interrupted,

"Comin' from Newcastle, the only border ah like is Hadrian's Wall, man."

The three of them laughed. Keith, glad to be away from the computer room he loathed. Near the door on the other side of the bar, Rick sat like a limpet to a rock, one hand on his half empty pint glass and the other holding a cigarette. Next to him, Dennis and Jeff were discussing where they should go that evening. From the back of the bar, where the dart boards and bar billiards were situated, came a lone voice. It was Brian from the overtime shift.

He sang, "Hi-ho," and faced the bar.

To his left side Glen got up and sang,

"Hi-ho."

Then, the rest of the overtime shift stood up, downed the remainder of their drinks in one gulp and followed Brian out of the bar singing,

"Hi-ho, hi-ho, it's back to work we go," looking nothing like Snow White's Dwarves.

This chorus prompted Blundon Transport III to start singing a variety of songs. In his usual effort to keep in with the lads, Eugene had got a big round in and shouts of "Careful." and "Don't drop it." had rung out as he had ferried the tray of drinks back to the gallant team. By three o'clock the bar had shut and in the surrounding room everyone was drinking up.

At four o'clock the Blundon boys were banging on the side of their mini bus whilst the Sulcrem lads were dancing an Indian rain dance around the vehicle. Bemused passers-by hurried passed thinking they may be asked to join a Hari Krishna sect and go off chanting down the high street.

Chapter 6

Leisure

Shift work gave our valiant band time off on different days of the week and so they had developed a routine of engaging in various leisure pursuits whenever possible.

On Monday morning Rick waited by his front room window, looking up and down the quiet side street he had lived in for the last two years. Although small, with two bedrooms, it was well built and near the local pub. Looking down to stub out his cigarette in the ashtray, he checked once again the bag of three golf clubs leaning against the windowsill.

His only sporting love was golf because it gave him the opportunity for fresh air, exercise and a large bag in which to carry lots of beer. Rick did not care about how many shots it took to reach each hole, rather how many cans per hole. Yes, he marked a score card but only on the amount of beer for a short course of nine holes.

The routine was the same each time: tee off, open can, start drinking, walk to ball sipping, can down, second shot, pick up can, walk to ball sipping – easy.

Jeff on the other hand was more competitive and hated to lose at anything. They played golf together once a week, weather permitting. Jeff had spent hundreds of pounds on his golf clubs and bag and studied golf videos to perfect his technique. When the two friends played it was a bit like Jack Nicklaus versus a mobile off licence.

In the distance Rick could see a shiny sports car approaching. He knew it was Jeff because the stereo was drowning out the engine noise with a version of 'When the Spurs Go Marching In'. As the car pulled as near to the front gate as possible, Rick wrestled the bag of beer and the three golf clubs outside.

Because of Rick's dedication to the sport they could only play on the public course a mile away. Jeff belonged to a private club but they had advised him not to bring his thirsty friend as he frightened the lady members.

Nearby, at the local gravel pit Dennis, Tim and Bruce were sitting a few yards apart fishing. Whenever they could, the three of them would spend hours pitting their wits against any coarse fish available. Ever since childhood Dennis had fished this pit. He had taken Tim and Bruce along as something new for them to do two years ago and they had gone regularly ever since.

Bruce enjoyed putting maggots on the hook and reminding them of the species he wanted to catch. Of course, it didn't always work and when that happened he blamed Tim for being ugly and scaring away the fish.

When the weather was warm and they were in the shade, cold drink and food to hand, nothing could take them away from their pastime. But if, as was often the case, it was chilly and the fish were scarce, then an earlier departure was taken.

The gravel pit was large and very deep in the middle. A day ticket could be bought, but these boys were all season ticket holders and enjoyed pursuing the large fish that had been caught at the pit. A few tricks were played when the fishing was slower and they all took it in good spirit as part of the fun. The only time it had nearly got nasty was the occasion when Bruce got up to play a fish and Tim had put a plastic, but realistic, dog turd on his seat. After the euphoria of catching and bragging about the biggest fish of the day Bruce heard Tim shout out,

"Eeeeegggghhhh. What's that on your chair Bruce?"

Looking at his seat Bruce immediately shouted,

46

"What have you done?" Tim then picked up the turd and said,

"Oh it's ok Bruce, it's not runny," and put his hand with the turd to Bruce's face.

Bruce squealed, "Aagghhh. Get away." and, in an attempt to get clear, tripped over Dennis's leg and fell into the water. He came out wet and angry and chased Tim round the gravel pit, but as laughter got the better of them both they gave up running around and slowly went back to fishing, after Bruce had changed into the spare trousers that he always took along with him just in case.

"I'll get you back for that, you little git," said Bruce.

Sadly, Tim knew he would, but hopefully not for a while.

Over at the seedy end of town Stuart, Barry and Charlie carried their small holdalls into a square, one storey, large-windowed building. The sound of clunking metal and grunting could be heard. There was an odour of stale sweat in the air. Several multi-muscled, unshaven men picked up various heavy objects, their tattooed arms growing with every lift.

In a small office an even bigger man sat at a desk wearing a T-shirt emblazoned with *Gino's Gym*.

"Hi Gino, got room for us today?" asked Barry.

"Plenty of room lads. Are you going to try the men's weights this time?"

His sarcasm raised a small grin from a few of the gym users. As Gino was twice their size and trained every day, the lads felt no need to indulge in any manly banter and just laughed off his comment.

They enjoyed the weekly gym session but tried not to get to know too many of the clientele as some of them were quite unsavoury. Only the previous week Charlie had overheard a conversation that included the statement,

"Chainsaw? Well, if someone comes at you with a chainsaw, just take your jumper off and wrap it in the blade mate."

Charlie had thought there was a slight flaw in this plan because, while you were removing your jumper, the chainsaw attacker could have chopped off your legs. However, he didn't venture to share this thought with the man who was still spouting off loudly about various ways to ward off attackers using clothes. They had already nicknamed this man 'Shooter' as a reference to another menacing conversation that had been previously overhead.

In a quieter corner of the gym Stuart, Barry and Charlie went about lifting what they could and trying to look as manly as possible. They looked hopefully in the large mirrors that were all around, as if this was the session that they would magically transform into Adonises. But, sadly, no.

Darts played a part in the curriculum of our intrepid band of fun brothers. Every month the company had a list of the different larger departments that were going to be putting out a team. Smaller departments merged together so that they could also be included. A mini league had evolved and anyone, old, young, male or female could play. Some took it more seriously than others, but as these were quite boozy affairs, the main motivation was that the company paid for the first two rounds of drinks.

Sulcrem House had a small bar and two dart boards. The computer department always had enough players for a match. Due to lots of practice they also had some very good marksmen and the best of all was Rick. He would give the lads playing him a five game start and still usually beat them. Eugene studied Rick while he played and he was his darts idol. As Eugene watched, Rick's very heavy darts would score ton after ton. Sometimes Rick had a dart that would hit the wire rim of the board and bounce out. Eugene would chuckle as Rick always pretended to volley it, football style, into an imaginary goal before the dart landed on the floor.

On one occasion, in an attempt to impress Rick during a match against the accounts department, Eugene tried copying Rick's pretend volley as a dart bounced out of the board and headed towards the floor in front of him. Not having Rick's prowess, Eugene swung his leg really hard pretending to get his foot as close to the falling dart as possible. Unfortunately for him, his foot and the dart connected and the dart went through his shoe into one of his toes. Eugene had given a loud squeal and everyone watching the match had fallen about laughing as he had limped away to the toilets, asking a chuckling Rick to get the dart out of his foot.

In the summer some of the lads played for a local cricket team called Chisham Green. Again, it was more about the socialising afterwards than the match, but a reasonable standard was achieved. The team did not have its own ground but used the large expanse of grass that constituted the local green.

Our intrepid bodybuilders, Stuart, Barry and Charlie were the mainstay of the regular team, but if they were short of a player, they would involve any of the computer lads who had a clue about cricket. Before the game, one of the perks for the players was to go round asking any bikini clad girls to move off the cricket area. This was a job only Stuart felt qualified to do, but he always had lots of helpers.

~~~~~~~~~~~~~~~

During the summer there would be an outing to Lords or The Oval. This would mean another trip to the joke shop by all who would be attending. Over the years, more and more joke shop products were taken to the matches. With beer served all day the tendency was to become very silly from lunchtime onwards.

On one occasion at Lords, Margaret Thatcher and Ronald Reagan emerged from the stand arm in arm and waving to the crowd. Some jeered, some cheered, some threw peanuts or similar. Margaret and Ronald carried on around the ground getting a good deal of attention and laughter.

When they had gone about ten yards, four males ran after them, one had a bald head with a small pork pie stuck to it, another had a pair of false breasts and a grass skirt, another had a massive false plastic bottom and it wiggled as he jostled forward. The last male didn't wear fancy dress but had eyes staring widely, looking around almost dazed. The mini procession got halfway around the ground and headed back to their seats.

Yes, it was the computer department's finest. Margaret and Ron were Tim and Bruce, Porkpie man was Dennis, the Hawaiian girl was Ravi and the mad staring one was Greg from the night shift who had stayed up and taken some amphetamines to keep awake.

Obviously, as they took their seats the crowd around them had sensed they weren't troublemakers and warmly smiled and clapped as they disrobed and changed back into ordinary cricket fans again.

Cricket matches against the Australians were always heated and hotly contested both on and off the pitch. In the queue for drinks after lunch Dennis could see a small Aussie approaching slowly, carrying a tray full of lagers. He was wearing a T-shirt with the words *Pommie Bastards* emblazoned across the front. Quickly Dennis said to Bruce who was queuing with him,

"Watch this."

As the Aussie got closer through the crowd Dennis, discreetly for a big chap, stuck out his foot and the unsuspecting victim fell over spilling his whole tray of drinks and acquiring a huge cheer from the surrounding crowd. The queue moved forward with England's pride intact and no culprits in the dock.

As usual, it had been a day of constant beer and boisterousness and a great day's cricket. On the way out of the ground the lads had chatted about how the crowd seemed to have responded to their dressing up and wondered if it may catch on. Drunkenly they had staggered to the nearest pub to discuss it.

~~~~~~~~~~~~~~

Although the political persuasions in the computer room were about 50% Tory, 50% labour, arguments were mainly restricted to tea breaks or lunch breaks.

To some, Prime Minister, Margaret Thatcher had worked wonders with inflation, budget deficits and industrial turmoil and Thatcherism was the way forward. To others, she had smashed the workers' union rights, abandoned the nationalized industries and created millions of jobless people. One day shift lunch break Stuart and Tim were playing Bruce and Charlie at pool when Stuart announced,

"Another ten years and I'll have paid off my mortgage."

"Nice one mate," said Jeff, a staunch Tory, like Stuart.

"Bloody Yuppie," joked Tim.

"Yea, you capitalist lackey," said a smiling Bruce.

"Oh trust you labourites to be against a bloke owning his own place. My uncle was able to buy his council house last month. No chance of doing that under your lot."

"Thatcher the milk snatcher," Tim called out in a reference to her stopping free school milk.

"Power to the people Comrade," said Jeff in an even louder voice, laughing.

"Hang on," Stuart said to Tim and Bruce, "you two were the highest earners for overtime this month. You made a packet. Your wealth is growing too."

"Yea, but we are paying loads of it back in tax," said Bruce, "Anyway, what about the 'all our industries'? It's all going abroad."

Charlie, who had been listening to both sides of the now, slightly heated, debate decided it was time to change the subject. He held up a picture from a newspaper of a topless model and said,

"See her?"

They all stopped squabbling and said, "Yes,"

"Well, I went out with her last week."

Looking disbelievingly Stuart said,

"What, you went out with her?" pointing to the newspaper.

"Yes," replied Charlie, "she's ringing me here in about five minutes."

"Blimey," said Jeff, "she looks amazing."

Charlie continued, "Sally's on her break at the moment so if the phone goes and it's for me and I'm not about will you answer it?"

"Yes, definitely," said Tim.

Charlie told the lads he was just popping out to the newsagent but would be back as quickly as he could for the call. Jeff patted him on the back as he left muttering, "Blimey," again.

A few minutes passed and the reception phone rang.

"Quick, it's Charlie's bird," said Bruce and they all rushed to the phone. Jeff got there first and picked it up and, in his best voice said,

"Hello, Computer Reception."

"Oh hello, I'm Carmen, is Charlie there please?"

"No, I'm sorry, he went out. He won't be long though," said a nervous, but excited Jeff. Before Carmen could speak again Jeff blurted out,

"We liked your picture in the paper."

Stuart, Tim and Chris started laughing.

"Oh well, I'm only round the corner, shall I come and show you a real-life pose?" she asked teasingly.

"What now?" said Jeff.

"Yes, no time like the present. Are your colleagues going to watch? I can hear them, I don't mind."

"Wow. Yes," said Jeff, "we'll wait in reception for you."

"I'll be right there," said Carmen.

Jeff then quickly explained to Stuart, Chris and Tim, "She's coming in here to pose topless right now."

"What? Nice one, Jeff," said Stuart.

A few minutes later a tall, black lady with big hair, clad in a long leather coat, with the collar up and wearing sunglasses, walked seductively into reception.

She said in a quiet, dusky voice,

"Are you the lads that want a real-life model to look at?"

"Yes please," said Tim, "come up to our rest room, it's quieter."

Carmen slowly and seductively followed them to the rest room where Eugene and Dennis were playing pool. Before they could ask who she was Carmen, keeping her back to them, started to undo her coat.

You could have cut the tension in the room with a knife.

She took off her sunglasses and in an even duskier voice said,

"I'm not wearing a bra."

She turned to face the lads. She seemed to have white breasts. Before they knew what was happening she took off her afro wig and said,

"You dirty bastards."

It was Charlie. He had set the whole thing up. The room erupted with laughter with Charlie's loud laugh drowning out the rest.

"Lucky we keep a few joke shop props here boys," he said. All thoughts of politics had gone.

"How do you do that lady's voice?" Jeff asked Charlie.

Before he could answer Stuart said,

"Come on Carmen, put your boobs away, time to get back to work."

~~~~~~~~~~~~

Sulcrem House bar was an institution with many frequent visitors. At lunchtime it was generally filled by AMO office workers and, of course, computer operators. It was run by Ted, an ex-army, grey-haired, short, but extremely stocky, barman.

Ted ran the bar in the daytime from twelve o'clock until three o'clock. He was quiet and usually didn't get involved with any excitement going on around him. He knew all the regular management staff and would exchange brief, but polite pleasantries with them, whilst remembering what they liked to drink before they had ordered it.

There would also be a good mix of female staff in the bar from time to time and of course, with his fantastic memory, Ted would know their favourite tipple.

He usually accepted a drink from patrons of his bar if asked and, when the bar was quieter, he would have a game of darts with the computer staff. Ted should have retired years ago, but wanted some extra cash and the bit of life that a small bar offered, along with a readily available supply of alcohol whenever he wanted it.

Between one and two he was ably assisted by Doreen, a large, kind-hearted lady in her fifties. She mostly collected the empty glasses and washed them up but could turn her hand to pulling pints if needed.

If Doreen was unavailable and Ted was a bit rushed, any of the available computer lads would help behind the bar for ten minutes or so knowing Ted would give them a free pint later.

Normally, the bar ran without a hitch with darts matches and the fruit machine being occasionally played by the younger members of staff.

The managers, in suits, sat around the tables, in quiet solitude, smoking cigarettes, cigars and even a pipe in one case.

A far cry from the gathering of computer operators who would be telling jokes amid raucous laughter that they would try to tone down befitting the time of day.

In the evening things called for a slightly more outgoing staff to run the bar. That's where Orlando, the evening barman, came in. Tall, slim, short dark hair, with eyes a bit like a gecko, but baggier. No one knew his age but a guess would put him around forty-five. Openly gay and proud of it, he drank Bacardi like water and the occasional sniffing noises, out of sight at the back of the bar, suggested he also liked other forms of stimulants.

Not only did he encourage the computer operators to help behind the bar, he insisted that they did. That way he was free to sing loudly or dance and prance about in the way only he could.

Friday evenings would start quietly around 5.30 but, by seven o'clock, when the managers had all gone home, any rules would go out the window. There would be a few office workers drinking alone, not yet ready to go home, interspersed with some computer programmers and engineers, and the usual plethora of operators.

Behind the bar, out of sight, Orlando had his own cupboard where he kept a selection of hats and other accessories.

It wasn't unusual to see Stuart behind the bar with a flashing lamp sellotaped to his head, and Dennis, at the end of the bar, wearing the kaftan and slippers he had brought to wear on nights. In fact, Dennis had kaftans for the night and the day and every occasion.

Orlando would often be found in a Carmen Miranda headdress, dancing round the tables, flaunting himself at anyone interested. Being such an entertainer Orlando had his own music on a cassette tape blasting out from the bar. One evening Ravi had brought in some Indian music and Orlando had played it straight away. Orlando got as many people to the front of the bar as possible and Ravi proceeded to instruct them in how to dance Indian-style. Around the bar everyone copied him as best they could, with Orlando in his element dancing merrily behind the bar.

He had an agreement with the management that on darts evenings he wouldn't interrupt the flow of things, however, he still served at the bar dressed as the construction worker from *Village People*, his favourite band.

Orlando's pet hate was a quiet bar and he always tried to liven things up. One evening, things were very quiet by 7.30 and Johnny Cash was singing 'Ring of Fire' on the cassette tape. Orlando threw back his third double Bacardi, grabbed the cowboy hat from under the bar, poured lighter fuel over the top and set light to it. Almost possessed, with the flaming hat on his head he ran around the tables where people were sitting shouting "Don't panic. Don't panic."

At that moment Ivan, the security guard had popped in for a quick pint. On surveying the scene before him, he grabbed the ice bucket from the bar and threw it over Orlando's head, dousing the flames.

With a small amount of smoke rising from his hat Orlando shouted, "My hero," and tried to cuddle Ivan, but Ivan was too quick for him and headed out of the bar pronto.

If you drank in the Sulcrem House bar in the evenings you had to be ready for anything. It wasn't unusual for computer operators to go back to work or home from the bar doing a selection of Monty Python's silly walks, with anyone else welcome to join in.

Orlando's bar had the best bar takings of all the AMO's in-house bars around the country and he knew it. The only way that would change was if Orlando left and, despite all the antics, he knew his job was safe.

~~~~~~~~~~~~~

As they were on good salaries and the overtime was plentiful, about half of the computer operators had a house and a mortgage. The rest either rented a flat or were still living with their parents but intended to buy a house in the near future.

Among the current home owners, Keith (with his shift leader pay) was able to live a very good lifestyle. His house had been left to him by his parents and as they had been keen gardeners all their lives Keith had learnt well over the years. As the garden needed so much work to keep it in tip top shape he hardly ever did any overtime.

In the large back garden he had a summer house, a greenhouse, and a potting shed, along with a tool shed housing a mini ride-on mower. Once home, he didn't encourage visitors from AMO as he took his gardening and leisure time very seriously.

He had sculptured several hedgerows into shapes of animals, the lawn was immaculate and the area in front of the windows had a nice two-tone striping effect. There was a wild, but reasonably well-kept, area to one side of the garden with dozens of shrubs and flowers. Another part had fruit trees and a water feature stood as the centrepiece of the lawn. There were trellises, flower beds and a vegetable patch which, over the years had contained nearly every type of edible produce grown to a competition-winning standard.

Keith had often wondered what it would be like to run his own garden centre, but didn't want the hassle of doing so and, with his high salary, had decided to carry on working in computing, even though he didn't really enjoy it.

Rick had got his priorities right straight away; a house near a pub with a big enough kitchen in which to make homebrewed beer. It did have a spare bedroom but that was full of brewing accessories and glasses purchased at various beer festivals. He had acquired quite a collection from across the country.

Rick had converted the old shed in his garden into a mini bar and when the real pub was closed he could have a drink in his. A sign on the outside read *Abandon hope all ye that enter here*. Inside, at one end, there was a dartboard fitted on the wall at match height, well lit and with a floor mat marking out the throwing distances. Along the side wall was a hard-wearing bar top incorporating two taps for his home brew.

As Rick was an experienced home brewer he always had a barrel of ale ready to drink. He normally brewed beer for the barrel, but was also a dab hand at bottled beers.

On top of the bar there was a large ashtray and next to that a huge ghetto blaster available for listening to music, football or cricket matches or other live sporting events. On the wall above the bar was a neon sign displaying *Bar Open* and next to that, a poster displaying *Bar Rules:- if you're still standing, you need another drink*.

Several of the operators and pub regulars had visited Rick's shed and hoped it would be open for many years to come.

Stuart had owned his house longer than the others and had started to decorate every room but never quite finished any of them. He was great at fixing things and DIY, but just lacked the motivation to see the tasks through.

The front room contained very comfortable Chesterfield furniture but it was situated on top of a half-varnished wooden floor. A massive fish tank adorned one wall and was well filtrated and lit. Dozens of small colourful fish swam around. Above the fish tank were a couple of saucy paintings of scantily clad women.

Against the opposite wall was a state of the art turntable, amplifier and ridiculously loud speakers. The collection of blues and rock music was the envy of everyone who saw it. In the corner was a Wurlitzer juke box which also contained some amazing music. A silver glitter ball hung from the ceiling capturing the light and colours from all around.

Stuart's was usually the place to go for a good night in as, in the room next to the kitchen, there was a massive drinks cabinet which contained every spirit and liquor and was never unstocked. You could drink, smoke and wear whatever you liked, but only when Stuart's girlfriend was away overseas on one of her nursing contracts.

Dennis had a large house and, like Stuart, was very good at DIY. The difference was he always finished the tasks he undertook. The latest colour schemes, home-made furniture and everything in working order. He put all the years he had spent working on building sites before joining AMO to good use. He had watched electricians, plumbers and plasterers ply their trades and had gained a lot of practical knowledge.

Dennis had built his own mini cinema in one room. It had fake Roman columns and small theatre curtains that folded back when he was ready to watch a film. There was a row of five comfortable cinema seats he had bought at auction, a popcorn machine and a large fridge for drinks and snacks.

Dennis fixed everything whenever it needed it. He just loved to be busy. Putting his bricklaying skills to the test in the garden, he had made a semi-circular pond, three feet high and three feet deep. Large koi carp swum about in immaculately clear water. As some of the fish were very expensive he kept nets over the water to keep herons and other predators away.

Next to the pond a large double shed held fishing accessories, gardening and electrical tools, cement mixers, and other building equipment. Dennis was determined to stay single but, on seeing his household skills, his girlfriend was constantly trying to get him to pop the question.

Although the operators thought of Jack as a hippy he was also savvy enough to have bought a small house of his own. A rich aunt who had always worried about him, had left him enough money for a large deposit on a house with small monthly mortgage payments.

Art was his passion and he had been drawing and painting since he was a very young child. He specialized in geometric shapes and a clever use of colours, but could also paint people, buildings and landscapes. All the rooms in the house contained his artwork.

A lover of herbs and fresh vegetables he had started to grow them in his garden and, over time, had become very proficient at it. A staunch vegetarian, he prided himself on not using any pesticides and grew everything organically.

Despite his hippy outlook, loving people like he did he didn't want to stay at home on the dole. He wanted to work and be useful, earn money and engage with humans whenever possible, even if they didn't necessarily understand him, which happened quite a lot.

Barry's dad had been a mechanic and had taught him lots of practical skills. In buying his house he had been swayed by one that had a large double garage. Barry found he spent more time in there than the house. Tidily arranged around the walls were spanners and a wheel brace, different jacks, a compressor, paint spraying equipment, several tyres and lots of spare parts. A huge workbench and a couple of metal vices took up one wall and one half of the garage was occupied by an Escort Mexico rally car that Barry was renovating. Barry could be relied on if your car needed fixing in an emergency, but he tried not to help out his friends and colleagues too often, as he would never get anything else done.

Ben's house had an interesting garden. It wasn't overlooked, as the land behind was awaiting development and was standing empty. He made use of this opportunity as he loved to shoot powerful air rifles at small targets and had set these up at the end of the garden in front of the empty land. Axe marks in the trees, indeed, axes, knives, and kung fu stars in the trees, were all part of his dangerous outdoor activities. A large circular target was positioned next to the smaller ones in readiness for the arrows he shot from a powerful crossbow. His two Alsation dogs were free to roam the garden and knew to keep still whenever Ben was practising. Ben had had several girlfriends but still hadn't met one that appreciated his lifestyle.

Jeff, another skilled DIY exponent, had a large well-equipped house with the latest TV and video gadgetry, together with a garage for his relatively new car. In the very large bathroom he had installed a sauna, big enough for two people. Being a shift worker he couldn't always get to the public sauna at convenient times so this solved the problem for him.

Tim had converted his basement room into a music studio and, with the help of Dennis and Jeff, had soundproofed it. There were a couple of acoustic guitars, three electric ones and several amps, although some worked better than others. At the back of the room was an old drum kit, a bass guitar and three microphones. A couple of times a month he would get together with Jeff, Ben and Charlie for a jam session. Charlie had suggested that they try out some Ska music tracks and play in a pub, but actually committing to it was another matter. They usually got drunk and played punk rock, with Charlie portraying a very amusing version of Johnny Rotten.

Eugene, still living with his parents, had a large bedroom covered in pictures of space. When he was seventeen his dad had given him a CB radio set but he had recently upgraded to some musical broadcasting equipment and was known as DJ Clumsy Boy until the authorities had shut him down. When asked about getting his own place where he would have to cook, wash and clean, he always said, "No rush, no rush."

Bruce also had his own place near to the other lads. He had all the usual mod cons but in one of the rooms he had tanks of exotic creatures; lizards, dwarf frogs, small snakes and toads. They all had names and were treated very well.

Bruce was always looking to add to his collection and would avidly read the latest magazines for information.

Charlie had a bungalow which hadn't needed much refurbishment when he bought it. Although the rooms were small, it was enough for him. The old shed in the garden gave him the space he needed for the photographic hobby he was becoming increasingly good at. He had attended a couple of courses at the local night school and was progressing very well indeed. Obviously, being a budding video cameraman, this was another string to his bow. Charlie had thought about possibly branching out into wedding photography, or even sports pictures, but for the time being he was happy to carry on at an amateur level.

So, outside of work all of our group of operators led happy, normal and reasonably sensible lives. It was only when they all got together and large amounts of alcohol were involved that the silly season commenced. On organized nights out, or daytrips, nothing really strange happened without alcohol.

As far as they all knew, none of them had any fears or phobias except Eugene who, following an incident at his secondary school with a Ouija board in a dark classroom, one winter lunchbreak, was known for his fear of the occult. Sometimes at work he would speak to Sally about his fears as she was a good listener.

Eugene was telling Sally about the problems he had at home with the neighbours. His family were really scared and were being intimidated by the family that had recently moved in next door. They had offered to buy Eugene's house so they could have the area to themselves and when Eugene's dad had refused, things had started to get nasty. Excrement through the letter box, small stones thrown at the windows at night, loud music playing continually, and verbal abuse hurled at Eugene's family whenever they were outside in the garden. They were also warned that if they went to the police to report the abuse they would be physically harmed. Sally felt really sorry for Eugene and decided to tell their colleagues about his problems.

The word was passed around via the shift bush telegraph and Stuart asked anyone interested in helping Eugene to let him know. It didn't take long before he had fifteen names and a few very illegal suggestions as to what to do with the bullies.

Stuart, Dennis, Ben, Charlie, Rick and Barry decided that special tactics would be required and, between them, they started to hatch a plan. Tentatively Eugene agreed to gratefully accept their offer of help. The rest of the operators were informed and decided to meet at Rick's house as the barrel of beer at Stuart's had run out.

After they had been over the plan and everyone knew what was required of them, the lads went off to prepare. There was a hive of activity, with various comings and goings, but eventually everything was in place and Operation Exterminate was ready to roll.

The doorbell rang at the house next door to Eugene's family. A large, overweight, unshaven man in a vest and jeans and aged about sixty, opened the door and stared out menacingly. On the doorstep Stuart was standing clad in a black t-shirt, leather waistcoat and black jeans. Beside him, Ben was dressed in exactly the same attire. Behind them stood a large black lady wearing a colourful head scarf and long flowing dress. On seeing the man at the door she shook a maraca, swayed from side to side and gave a low moan.

"Good afternoon, Sir, have you ever considered the dark side?" asked Stuart.

"What?" came the reply.

"Ah, well some of us here hold a weekly meeting and we feel very good afterwards."

"Don't like all that religious mumbo jumbo," the man said.

Ben said "Mumbo Jumbo, we do that."

"What?" asked the man.

63

Stuart explained they had all been greatly helped in their lives by this new found teaching. The lady behind him shook the maraca and moaned again, swaying from side to side.

"Who is that?" the man asked.

"This is High Priestess Potti Nu Nu from Haiti. She is very gifted and sees much more than we do," Stuart replied.

By now the man's wife had also come to the front door and, as she stood behind him, the light from the hallway was blocked out.

"Clear off." she shouted.

"Be careful, don't offend the priestess," said Stuart.

"Look, piss off before I get my two sons out here." the woman said.

The priestess lurched forward, gave a deathly stare and ran her index finger across her throat.

Stuart said "Oops. You've done it now. She's going to put a voodoo curse on you."

"What a load of crap. Do your worst." the woman exclaimed, pulling her husband back out of the way and slamming the door.

Next door, in Eugene's garden, Dennis and Jeff had been busy erecting a wooden X-shaped structure, surrounding it, lying on the ground, were about a dozen black drain pipes with large flowerpots stuck on the ends. In the dark they looked like Swiss alpine horns.

The two houses were situated at the end of a cul-de-sac with a small copse behind, so nothing going on in the rear gardens could be seen by anyone else.

A variety of noises could be heard coming from the wooded area at the back of the garden. Electric cables led from Eugene's house to Stuart's very loud speakers which had been positioned, out of sight, in the small wood.

At dusk a corn dolly had been stuck on Eugene's neighbours' door and the doorbell rung. Once more, the senior male occupant of the house opened the front door. No one was there so he walked outside and shouted out,

"Show yourself."

On the way back to the house he spotted the corn dolly on the front door. By now, the rest of the family had come out to see what was going on. In the distance an eerie voice called out,

"Beware of the dead cockerel," and faded away.

One of the younger males, started to get agitated and said,

"We ain't scared of no bloody cockerel." and he and his brother started to walk down the path to see who was about.

On finding nothing untoward they returned to the house and shut the front door. Immediately, all the electricity in the house went off and the lights went out. The windows at the rear of the house had been daubed with fake blood. Jack had been busy painting by torchlight.

A variety of weird noises could be heard from the front and rear of the house. Whirring, anguished clucking, and banshee howls.

By 11.30, with the electricity still not working and no more noise, the bullies decided to go to bed and sort everything out in the morning. They didn't seem so arrogant now and the younger males took baseball bats upstairs with them.

At 12.30 the bullies were woken by the sound of beating drums and a mass of flames flickering in the next garden. A twelve-feet high wooden X-shape was on fire. In front of that there was a three-feet high cockerel rising from an egg.

From nowhere, fourteen shapes in cloth sacks started dancing and chanting around the fire. Haunting drum beats came from behind. Two devil dogs sat on guard either side of the cockerel. Then, through a gap in the fence where a panel had been removed, Potti Nu Nu entered the garden from the copse at the back. Swaying and spitting water onto the fire and shaking a maraca, she started undulating and writhing as the drums got louder.

Suddenly, a cloud of yellow smoke (from ten smoke bombs that had been let off in the woods) engulfed the cockerel and both it and the devil dogs disappeared. When the smoke cleared Potti Nu Nu, her eyes bulging, was holding up a small plastic chicken by the neck and pointing towards the bullies' house.

At that moment the fourteen sack cloth-adorned disciples picked up the drainpipes or fake Swiss alpine horns and stood in a circle around the flames. They all blew in time. A haunting, singular note.

Scary howls emanated from the woods and then, as they faded, a bell could be heard tolling loudly. Rick had an empty beer barrel and a lump hammer.

One of the younger bullies had quickly got dressed and ran out of the front door, only to be met by Ben.

"Out of my way, Shortie," the bully said.

"Can't do that," said Ben.

"I can't fight midgets," said the big man.

With this, Ben kneed him in the crutch and the bully fell to his knees.

"Now you can," said Ben and proceeded to knock seven bells out of him.

The bully's brother ran down the stairs to help but Ben called out,

"Fluffy, Quentin," and two large Alsations appeared beside him growling.

The operators then stormed through the door and, in a matter of minutes, the four bullies were wrapped up and mummified in thick sellotape and placed in a circle in the front room, with tape covering their mouths.

Stuart said, "The moon is high and the magic strong. You have one chance or you will die."

The bullies, eyes staring, felt totally helpless.

"Will you lick the toad's head in an effort to appease the spirit god, Bla and live?"

All four heads nodded thinking, "A toad, how hard can that be?"

Potti Nu Nu brought in the first toad. It was a Colorado river toad, one of four that Barry had. She held the toad high in the air and the devotees started chanting,

"Um bla, Um bla."

The gags were removed and she held the toad up for the first of the bullies to lick. She got a fresh toad for the next person and so on. All the while, the chanting continued.

What the bullies didn't realise was these were toads that make you hallucinate and see all sorts of things. Within five minutes the effects were obvious and they spent the next hour on a very powerful trip. During that time they confessed to numerous crimes and admitted that had they been able to purchase Eugene's house it would have been part of a drug growing operation. This confession was filmed by Charlie, or Princess Potti NuNu as he was now known.

An agreement was reached that they promised to leave Eugene and his family alone and to move away or the tape recording of their confession would go to the police.

By morning no trace of anything was visible in the garden except for some smouldering ash. Dennis had collected the drainpipes. Jeff had his Spurs cockerel back in his garden. Ben's two dogs had enjoyed a great night out. Rick's beer barrel was back in his shed and the toads had been returned to Barry's contact who traded in dodgy reptiles. Nothing was ever seen again of the bullies. They didn't even return for their belongings.

~~~~~~~~~~~~

There was a smell of toast in the air. Someone was calling out.

"Eugene, Eugene, come on, you've got work in an hour."

A bleary-eyed Eugene looked up and watched his mum put a tray of tea and toast down on the bedside table.

"You were calling out earlier dear."

"What did I say?" Eugene enquired.

"Oh something like, 'Um bla, Um bla'. I don't know.

"Thank God. It was all a dream," thought Eugene, "but it has helped, I don't feel scared any more."

He had no more nightmares about the occult from then on.

Chapter 7

Holiday

Most of the computer staff enjoyed a couple of holidays a year and the extra money earned in overtime usually covered this. This year, Barry, Jeff and their girlfriends had decided to go on a walking holiday. Being quite fit and experienced walkers, they thought they would try and walk one of the Cornish coast paths, with some nice scenery and a sprinkling of pubs to tempt them. They planned to walk about ten miles a day, find a campsite to pitch their tents for the night and move on in the mornings.

Barry had found out which campsites to head for and planned a daily route. The train from Paddington would take them to Plymouth in enough time for them to head for Polperro to set up the tents. Jeff's girlfriend, Brenda was a nurse and so no stranger to keeping going for hours on her feet. Barry's girlfriend, Sheila, was a hairdresser and also used to standing all day. So, this week should pose no problems for any of them. Of course, the girls would be reminding their beloveds that they would also be having two weeks abroad on a lazy holiday this year as well.

After a pleasant journey down on the train with several alcoholic beverages consumed by all, our West Country travellers left the train at Plymouth in a happy mood. With rucksacks on, walking boots tightened up, and a purposeful stride, they got to the campsite in good time. The tents were put up in impressive style and off they went to the nearby pub for a few more drinks and an evening meal.

Chatting to a few locals they shared a few jokes and were made most welcome. They received advice from their newly found friends about good pubs and food along their route. Barry knew it was unlikely they would get to visit all of them but thanked his fellow drinkers on the way out.

When they got back to the tents, the campsite was fairly full with other campers: camper vans in one part and tents in the other. The following morning, after a good night's sleep, Jeff had got up for a much needed walk over to the toilet block when he spotted a familiar car in the car park, containing what looked like four corpses. As he got closer he recognized the faces. Smiling, seeing that it was Stuart, Charlie, Tim and Rick he instantly seized the opportunity for a surprise. He went right up to the car and shouted,

"Cornish Police. You're nicked. Out of the car now."

Eyes started to flicker inside the car when Jeff shouted again from behind the vehicle,

"Put your hands where we can see them." As four sets of hands slowly went up Jeff shouted,

"Cornish police. You are surrounded. Out of the car now."

He stayed crouched behind the rear of the vehicle as four, tired looking men got out of the car, arms up, wondering why the police were so good at camouflage.

"Jump up and down," Jeff shouted. Scared, they did so.

"Turn around. Keep turning." Jeff had them doing 360° turns and when he thought they were giddy enough he stood up and said,

"Come on you Spurs."

Stuart, suddenly realizing he knew the voice, looked at Jeff and called him a few choice names. The others joined in with similar insults. Then they all started laughing.

"What the hell are you lot doing here?" Jeff asked.

Rick explained that they had been planning to have a week off boozing and lazing about at home but on a whim

70

had driven down through the night to meet up, as Barry had said where they would be starting from.

"Wait", said Jeff, "You drove all night from London. How much sleep have you had?"

"Well, Stuart and Charlie slept most of the way and Tim and I stayed awake sharing the driving."

"Got much camping gear?" Jeff then asked.

"None," said Rick. "We're staying in pubs or B&Bs along your route. Just tell us where you will be at the end of each day and we'll meet up."

"Nice one, OK," said an impressed Jeff. He showed them on their map where the campsite was that they would be staying that night.

"See you later, hopefully," said Jeff as they drove off and four waving hands emerged from the car windows. One of the hands then changed to a peace salute the wrong way round, moving in an up and down motion.

Later that morning, Jeff told his fellow campers of his chance meeting earlier. The girls seemed a bit apprehensive but were reassured by Barry that it wouldn't affect their holiday. They all spent the rest of the day enjoying the coastal scenery, stopping for a drink and a pasty at lunchtime, then onto the campsite to pitch the tent.

As Barry was paying the nightly fee in reception, the site manager informed him that a message had been left for them. He handed Barry a note of the telephone call and on his way back to the tents, Barry read the message.

"Will be in the *Blue Budgie* tonight. Come and have a pint. Stuart."

Barry had already seen where the *Blue Budgie* pub was situated during the earlier walk to the campsite. He told the others and it was agreed they would all meet up later.

An hour later, Jeff went to the fish and chip shop to get supper for them all. After all the Cornish air and a good meal they decided the first day of the holiday had been great.

71

They left for the pub at seven o'clock and on entering, immediately spotted the four individuals gathered around the pool table. Jeff said,

"Oh look, it's the Booze Brothers."

Stuart, Rick, Tim and Charlie looked up and exchanged pleasantries and a bit of lively banter, Jeff got in a round of drinks and the evening commenced.

Stuart suggested the girls had a game of pool together as he had been playing on the table since 5.30. The lads all stood up at the bar and began chatting with the barman. He had found out about the lads' liking for practical jokes and about half way through the girls' game of pool, as Brenda was about to take her shot, released from the ceiling a large plastic spider on a piece of string. Brenda and Sheila both screamed and the bar erupted with laughter. The chuckling barman told them they get all the non-locals with that spider. He also mentioned that in Cornwall, tourists were known as grockles.

The evening was going well and some local lads came in and got chatting and enjoying some banter with the latest influx of grockles. They warmed to Charlie straight away as he told them he was from Iceland but had just come from a week in the Scilly Isles, which accounted for his great colour.

The locals told them about a cider festival taking place the next day, about four miles away. As it was just off the coast path Jeff and Barry were keen to attend. They just had to persuade the girls. Stuart's group had already said they would be there, no problem.

As they left the pub at closing time Rick said,

"See you at lunchtime."

"Lunchtime?" said Sheila.

"Ah, yes the cider thing," said a tentative Barry. Before she could say any more he said, "Only a couple. You both like cider don't you?"

"Yes, just a couple though," Brenda pitched in.

"OK. Sorted," said Jeff.

The next morning our intrepid walkers made excellent time and got to their lunchtime stop with time to spare. The pub with the cider festival wasn't even open yet so they went down to the sea for a swim and a sunbathe.

Walking back to the pub they saw a group of men shuffling around anxiously, waiting for it to open. On closer inspection the men again, had familiar faces.

Charlie, on seeing them said in a loud voice

"This is where the AA meeting is being held right?"

This brought laughter from everyone and any awkwardness the girls had about meeting up swiftly disappeared.

At noon sharp the pub doors opened and an extremely large, red-faced man in his fifties greeted the ensemble with,

"Take it easy on the *Sirens' Ruin*, you'll get wrecked."

A slightly surprised Stuart said,

"OK we will."

As they went in to the side room that was laid out for the cider festival the girls remarked on what a nice pub it was, while the lads studied how strong the barrels of cider were.

In an act of harmony they let the girls choose the first drinks. They were advised by the friendly bar staff to have half pints as the cider was quite strong. After about four drinks from different orchards everyone started feeling a different perspective on life.

Folk music started up with two local musicians. The voices got louder in the room and there was a lively atmosphere. By now, Barry and Jeff were sitting around a table with Brenda and Sheila while the others stood at the bar chatting to several locals.

The man on the door who had let them in had just got his first cider and asked the lads what they thought of it all. Rick had his happy drinking face on and said,

"Love it. Love the cider, love the people."

The others all agreed and they got another round in. It turned out the man on the door was called Kitto and he also owned the pub. He was joined by a very stocky, large-bellied man, about the same age.

"This is Jago, my younger brother." Kitto announced. "Don't talk to him. He's the village idiot."

Smiling, Jago retorted with,

"Idiot? Me? He spent two weeks studying for a urine test."

The stage was set. Kitto had to respond,

"You're such a little turd, when you sit on the beach cats try to bury you."

Laughter now resounded all around the bar. More cider, accompanied by the occasional pasty, and lively banter between the locals and the visitors, all made for a convivial atmosphere.

While the folk musicians had a break, a few stories were told. Kitto had started a round of bar jokes with,

"What do you call a woman who is always hanging out washing?"

"Peggy." shouted Jago and everyone laughed.

"A snake slithers into a pub and goes up to the bar. The landlord says 'I'm sorry, I can't serve you'. 'Why not?" asks the snake. 'Because you can't hold your drink."

Howls of laughter to Stuart's turn at joke telling.

Charlie said,

"I went to my doctor and asked if he had anything for persistent wind. He said 'yes' and gave me a kite."

Several more jokes were shared. One of the locals had started to talk about cremation and in a loud voice Kitto said,

"We'll put all talk of cremation on the back burner."

In their state of intoxication pretty much anything that was said was funny to our cider enthusiasts.

Thanks to the special licence Kitto had obtained, he could stay open till four o'clock and, with an hour to go until then, the sea of scrambled brains and reddish faces were starting to lose their reason.

Finally Kitto decided it was time for the *Sirens' Ruin* and he produced a small barrel. Pricey, it was only for the chosen few, which meant anyone in the area of the bar. The two musicians had apparently been drinking it on their break. One of them had plugged in his electric guitar and, abandoning the folk music, started the second set with a heavy metal medley. The audience loved it.

One half of *Sirens' Ruin* on top of several other ciders was too much for an elderly local man and he was carried out by Kitto and Jago to a waiting taxi.

Two people had been sick and one of the toilets was out of order. Kitto seemed unconcerned, however, and continued to help any one that needed it on their way out.

Barry and Jeff had been drinking at a much slower pace like the girls. However, as soon as they had consumed half a *Sirens' Ruin* they became whirling dervishes as the musicians played louder and heavier. When the music eventually stopped, to rapturous applause, the girls helped the boys on with their rucksacks ready for the stagger to the campsite.

Barry sat on a low wall outside the pub and laughed so much (at nothing at all) that he fell off the wall and landed on his back with the rucksack beneath him, still attached to his back. He looked like the happiest dying fly you have ever seen as his arms and legs flayed about while he still laughed his head off.

It was decided that rather than go straight to the campsite it would be better to head to the beach for a nap in order to sober up. Their last vision of the pub was of Kitto and Jago jousting with two small potted cactus plants, in a re-enactment of a medieval battle, chanting Anglo-Saxon words at each other.

On reaching the beach Charlie and Rick fell fast asleep as soon as they lay down on the sand. The girls sat watching as one of the locals tore off his clothes and ran into the sea to perform a drunken front crawl which lasted two strokes then petered out. They continued watching as he emerged from the water a moment later, staggering about trying to find his clothes.

A short time later Brenda and Sheila also drifted off to sleep while the loud snoring and alcohol fumes emanating from Charlie and Rick discouraged any sea birds from the vicinity.

For the rest of the week more pasties, cream teas, fish and chips, beer, and cider were consumed. As the coast path was quite steep in parts and they were each carrying a rucksack, they got fitter each day setting a good pace on the daily hikes. By the end of the week everyone was much fitter and had gained a healthy colour.

Chapter 8

The Outing

Over the course of the next month the talk on all the shifts was about the forthcoming trip to Lincoln. Ralph, the operations manager, had made several checklists and a running order. Most of the computer department would be going on the trip but the few that were not meant there would be enough staff to man the department in their absence.

Stuart had insisted on his boys going to the joke shop for a variety of performance-enhancing props for the day's mayhem.

Sally had opened a letter from brewery owner, Mr Ruttle, saying all was ready for their visit and she had gone to the train station to collect a batch of return tickets to Lincoln.

On Wednesday morning memo number 421 arrived from Ralph saying any dangerous horseplay or wanton vandalism during the outing would be greeted with instant dismissal. Naturally, everyone responded with hearty laughter upon reading this.

By Thursday most of the computer department's workload had been undertaken and distributed to all the departments. Patrick from Salaries had made sure there were no problems with the payslips as a rerun of the job would cause a minor panic at this stage. Our gallant band needed their money, as less money could result in a lacklustre outing, which would be no good to anyone.

On Friday the programming department took bets on how many people would fail to get back from the trip. Cliff, who managed the Times crossword in twenty minutes was favourite with five.

Saturday morning a growing number of people gathered at Kings Cross Station. Needless to say Ralph was the first there at 6.30 a.m. The rest started to arrive by about seven o'clock. Most carried plastic bags or holdalls containing everything from beer and sandwiches to plastic false breasts and more outrageous paraphernalia.

Stuart's shift waited patiently together for the first of the special guests to arrive. One guest per person was the rule, but by the time they all boarded the train it would be too late to notice that there were far more than that.

Two hulking, unshaven men, hands in pockets, walked menacingly toward the group from the computer department. Their six feet plus frames jostled through the crowd to reach Bruce, from Stuart's shift, who had invited them. He was not even slightly startled when they grabbed his legs and put him on their shoulders nor when they jumped up and down with him. When they had put him back to earth Bruce said,

"This is Roy," putting his hand on Roy's shoulder, "and this is Alan. Two of my gentlest friends."

This was met with laughter from the surrounding group.

Just then, Sally arrived along with four of her friends from her aerobics class. All conversation stopped. Sally wore a pair of jeans and a T-shirt that must have been painted on. Her friends wore miniskirts, leggings and shorts and they all looked voluptuous. En masse the crowd of day trippers, eyes not moving, shuffled towards them. Several of the lusty lads wanted to get in the first word and a verbal free-for-all ensued.

"Lads, lads," Sally shouted, "these are my friends. Kathy-" As Sally pointed to the raven-haired beauty, Tim shouted,

"I love you." Kathy laughed but looked down, coyly.

"This is Chrissy, Sheena and Ros," Sally continued. When she got to the last one a loud cheer went up and everyone started singing,

"We love you Ralph, oh yes we do, we love you Ralph, oh yes we do."

Ralph, blushing slightly, started to wave his arm towards the platform, checking the first five people. As everyone realised the ticket barrier was now open, they swept passed him, leaving him to stumble into the ticket collector's booth.

A garbled message came over the station tannoy about the special train to Lincoln: charter service only. Knowing there would be a bar on the train, Rick beckoned his shift colleagues to a compartment near the back of the ageing train. During the next few minutes Sally's carriage was packed. The lads stood around in any available space, knowing the view inside was far better than the one outside.

"Move along please," said a railway official, checking tickets.

Groans of disapproval could be heard amongst the slow-moving procession. When everyone had found a seat and all the tickets had been approved, the guard signalled to the driver to start the journey.

Slowly, the train edged its way forward. A voice in the distance called out,

"Hang on Man. Wait for me."

It was Jack, the cleaner, sprinting towards the back of the train. On hearing him, Ben pushed the window down and leaned out. Waving to Jack to keep going he opened the door and grabbed his outstretched arm, pulled him in and then shut the door.

"Great, nice one," said Jack as he was handed a beer from Rick for his trouble.

Stuart stood up and handed beer around from his bag and said,

"This is until the bar opens. Cheers lads," taking several gulps from the can he belched loudly and sat down. For the next few minutes elbows were raised and heads tipped back. Breakfast was consumed.

As for the rest of the train, there was not a single carriage where an alcoholic drink had not been opened. Not bad for 8.15 in the morning.

During the next hour, with the bar now open, people were merrily moving up and down the train to see who was sitting where. By now, some of the joke shop items were in use. The guard walked through the train and saw several plastic bald heads with a variety of coloured hair around the sides. He saw people wearing false breasts and bottoms, false beards and even a chef's hat. Losing track of how many tins of beer he had been offered, he sighed and thought,

"This could get out of hand."

Like a Second World War Spiv, Rick went around giving out the forged tickets for free beer at the brewery. He made sure that no one told Captain Sensible. Word had reached Stuart that their gallant organiser didn't plan to drink until much later in the day. Something must be done about that, he thought and walked down through the train to see Sally and her friends. He explained to the girls that if they didn't get Ralph drunk, half of the things that had been planned for the day would be stopped before they got going. The girls decided Sheena was the ideal candidate to trap the dedicated, single, Operations Manager into a day of monumental intoxication. Being a slightly built, blue-eyed blonde, full of fun, with a stream of past dodgy relationships, and currently unattached, she agreed.

Sally introduced them and asked Ralph if he would keep an eye on Sheena as she was a bit shy and scared of large groups. Sheena and Ralph sat in the empty carriage caused by Ralph's charisma and exchanged stories and tales of woe. Sheena, totally convincing, explained how she liked the idea of a good day out but wasn't sure about all the drinking. Ralph, trying to bring this shy little wallflower (or so he thought) out of her shell, said a few drinks could be fun. Sheena asked if it was true that he was afraid to let his hair down.

"Of course not," Ralph asserted.

"Well, you're not wearing anything silly or drinking, are you?" Sheena taunted. She picked up her bag and handed Ralph a plastic trick bone.

"Put this on your nose," she instructed.

Ralph looked embarrassed then added,

"Well, you aren't wearing anything silly or drinking, either."

Sheena handed him a can of lager and coaxed,

"Tell you what ... Let's push the boat out and each have a lager."

He looked relieved at not being asked to do anything daft and was happy to say,

"Ok, why not?"

During the course of the next hour she kept producing various items for him to wear, thus making him drink faster. He wanted to appear to be letting his hair down. Stuart made sure the twosome were kept supplied with drink and, minute by minute, Captain Sensible was becoming Captain Insensible. But due to Sheena's cunningly good company Ralph didn't realise what was happening.

So far, things were going to plan. Stuart had received reports of raucous singing, a streaker, a shaving foam fight and the news that someone had already been sick. What a day they were in for and it was only 9.45, half an hour's travelling yet until Lincoln.

At the front of the train Eugene, the shift Jonah, started a game of Grand Prix Winner. This entailed shaking a large can of beer and pulling the ring pull, then spraying everyone with the contents. One problem with his plan: he had decided to soak Ben, Barry, Bruce, Roy and Alan. They waited for his can to subside, Bruce then pulled Eugene to the floor and Ben produced a large roll of Sellotape. Eugene would be familiar with it as a similar roll had secured him to the chair in the shower the previous month.

When Eugene's feet were wrapped, they continued on up to his knees then suspended him, upside down, from the luggage rack. Thinking this was all that was going to happen, Eugene laughed. But when Bruce's large friend, Alan, produced a small water-filled fire extinguisher from his bag, Eugene squealed. A sharp bang of Alan's fist and the seal was broken. Water flowed freely over Eugene's feet, down his jeans and shirt and dripped from his head. Ben and Barry shouted,

"Fire, fire," but poor old Eugene just shouted.

In his tiny compartment the guard sat on the floor with his feet on the door repeating the words,

"Saturday overtime, never again."

The one and only time he had ventured up and down the train he had been hit on the back of the head with half a pork pie.

"Who did that?" he had exclaimed, turning around into a stream of party poppers, silly string, and some shaving foam.

Running back to his compartment he had bumped into special guest, Dave. Moving aside, the intrepid guard slipped on the unwanted contents of someone's stomach. Picking himself up from the floor and now covered in plastic string, shaving foam, bits of pie, and vomit he edged hopelessly back to his compartment. By now the train was strewn with foam, beer cans, cigarette butts, Sellotape, and a badly dented false bottom.

Further down the train, a conga had started to the tune of "Let's all go to Lincoln, let's all go to Lincoln la-la-lala-la-la-lala." Slowing down, the battered old train reached Lincoln Station amid cheers. Ralph, who hadn't moved throughout the journey, was still captivated by the lovely

Sheena. Unfortunately, he had drunk a lot more beer than was good for him, but didn't seem to care, as long as he didn't have to dress up.

Stepping off the train a sea of plastic bald heads, with bright hair at the side, false beards, men with plastic breasts and bottoms, all clutching beer cans and bleating like sheep, filed out of the station. The girls, merry, but reasonably sober, helped Ralph along the platform, telling him to enjoy himself.

Chapter 9

Lincoln

Being a large town with plenty of everything, Lincoln was the ideal choice for a large party of people with varied interests. Unfortunately, most of this group had only one thing in mind: a day's drinking and merriment.

Stuart had made sure the girls took Ralph away with some of their quieter colleagues and searched for the true Lincoln. Obviously, going to the odd pub on the way round would break up the day and Ralph for once, would do as he was directed. Sally arranged to meet everyone back at the station and took her detachment of ten semi-inebriates down the high street.

They only had an hour and a half until the brewery visit, so Rick was in a mild panic. He wanted to get to a pub near the brewery and quickly. Running to the mini cab rank he asked the driver,

"Can you quickly take us near Ruttle's Brewery, mate?"

"Yes, how many of you?" the cabby enquired.

Rick looked round,

"About sixty-five," he advised, waving to them all to come over.

"I'll take four, the rest behind," the cabby pointed to a row of six cars queuing for passengers.

"Have to radio in for backup."

Soon, every available cab in a ten mile radius of Lincoln was heading for the station.

It was only about a ten minute drive to the *Flatulent Bullock*, a large pub situated almost opposite the brewery. Usually the trade didn't pick up on a Saturday until about one o'clock. A young, lone barman was on duty in the lounge having just served the only patron, a man with a bag of washing. Suddenly, a group of four, fairly tall, red-eyed men with bald heads, Castro beards, and carrying bags, burst through the main doors. Making straight for the bar, Rick shouted,

"Morning. Five pints of bitter, please. What are you lot having?"

As the bewildered chap started pouring the first pints, four more joke shop refugees rushed in. Then four more and so on. For twenty minutes the lounge filled with sixty-five beer gypsies, with exploding cigarettes, laughter and wind. They were in the pub for less than an hour but bar sales suggested around 150 pints of Ruttles bitter had been consumed. The barman had rung the brewery for extra help and to inform them what to expect for the next tour.

Mr Ruttle was the third generation of his family to run the brewery. An educated man, well dressed in a top drawer suit and with an accent to match. Although not a snob, he did keep himself and his wife and children apart from most ordinary folk. Able to afford the best schools, the best house, and the best car, he was a respected man around the area. He insisted on personally meeting all brewery visitors in order to give a good impression. Showing them that Thaddeus Ruttle was a man of his word.

Forming a line at the large iron gates displaying *Ruttle's Brewery*, and beginning, at last, to show signs of being slightly soused, the AMO mob awaited their guide.

Out of respect for the hallowed premises, Stuart and Rick removed their beards etc and the others all followed suit. From around the corner of the office block, a grey haired man, wearing a boiler suit, limped towards his guests. Surprised to find no one dressed up,

"I 'erd you were all bald," his local accent and attempt at humour, making the group all chuckle.

"You all cum inside an' meet Mr Ruttle," waving his arm to the front of the line to advance.

Lingering in the air was a smell that meant beer was being brewed. Walking towards them along the brewery yard, was a smartly dressed man in his fifties. A determined look on his face. Flashing a smile, he addressed the tour party,

"Welcome to Ruttle's, everyone. I'm Thaddeus Ruttle and this is George, our head brewer."

At this point he turned to George and waited for him to speak but all he managed was,

"I thought they were all bald Mr Ruttle."

Amid chuckling, the tour began. Facts and statistics were given during the next half hour and the group were well behaved. Rick thought,

"Perhaps a pint to walk round with? Oh well, won't be long."

They had been shown the hop store, the grain store, the large coppers, and the fermentation area. Just the barrelling and bottling plant left, then some free beer. Mr Ruttle had brought George in on the technical aspects of the science of brewing and with forty years' experience, he knew his stuff.

Mr Ruttle thanked George for sharing his knowledge, then asked,

"Does anyone have any questions?"

"Yes," hollered Juan, "Wat is de largest planet in de solar system?"

Mr Ruttle, appreciative of the humour, replied,

"Do I sense this tour party is getting thirsty?"

A resounding "Yeeesss" was the reply and the rest of the visit was speeded up.

On approaching the sampling room there was an air of quiet expectation. Opening the door and standing in front of it, Mr Ruttle directed,

"Now, you've all got your two free beer vouchers for two half pints, hope you enjoy it."

Little did he know they were armed with several free tickets.

At the small bar three wooden barrels saying *Mild, Best Bitter* and *Special Bitter*, beckoned like bright light to moths.

Charlie was the first to be served and in a deep, West Indian accent said,

"Gimme a rum and black please."

Going even paler than he already was, the barman stated,

"Sorry, only beer, Sir."

Reverting to his London accent Charlie joked,

"All right, 'alf of best then mate."

The ice had been broken and nothing else. Efficiently, everyone had their free half then another and another. Mr Ruttle looked at the clock above the bar and thought the tour should be finished drinking by now. Nevertheless, he went on mingling and sipping the same half pint.

Some of the helpers at the bar were getting suspicious and decided to see who was having more than they should. Tim, eyes glazed and smiling, was asked if two halves always affected him like that? Swaying to and fro he told one of the barmen that all his mates who couldn't come had given him their tickets. Similarly, everyone else who was questioned had the same answer.

Singing was now in full swing. Out came the Prince Charles' joke ears, the eyes on springs, and various masks. Mr Ruttle received reports of a streaker running round the brewery, alias special guest, Dave.

A decision was made to close the bar discreetly. Mr Ruttle cleared his throat and in his loudest voice announced,

"Thank you all for coming."

Nothing happened. He tried again. The singing continued.

Mr Ruttle went out of the door towards the offices. Returning a few moments later, carrying a megaphone, he enthused what great voices they had and hoped they had enjoyed the trip. This was greeted with a loud cheer which turned to a boo when it was announced the bar would have to shut to get ready for the next tour that was due to arrive shortly.

Mr Ruttle, feeling personally responsible for his tour parties, had laid on two coaches to take everyone back to the station. Once everyone was on board the singing started up again, with Mr Ruttle tentatively joining in with the songs he knew.

Back at the station, the taxi rank was now back to normal and the train schedule was still running on time.

Sally's group had been to a pub, a hologram exhibition, a pub, a funfair and a pub. Ralph had been encouraged to drink at every opportunity and had adopted the guise of a man with a speech impediment and increasingly wobbly legs: a bit like a newborn baby giraffe.

Ten minutes before the train was due to take them one stop down the line, an out of breath Dave slinked onto the platform. Managing to evade the brewery security guards he had got dressed behind a stack of barrels. He now sat on a bench waiting. Pausing thoughtfully, he mused how beer affected people, causing them to do all sorts of bizarre things.

Two coaches pulled into the station car park and a multitude of brewery pilgrims, led by a man in a suit, headed for the platform. Sally and friends arrived and were introduced to Mr Ruttle. Ralph tried to shake his hand but missed, mumbling inanely,

"I hope you had a great day."

Mr Ruttle, voice loud, but comforting, thought Ralph had a learning disability.

"Good bye everyone. Thanks for coming."

Stuart jumped across the platform.

"No wait Mr Ruttle. Let me shake your hand for your great hospitality."

Their train started to pull in and everyone began singing, "We love Ruttle's beer," over and over again.

Dozens of hands were thrust at the brewery proprietor. He couldn't shake them all. Noisily the train started filling up and Sally shouted from inside.

"Come and shake daft Ralph's hand again, please."

Doing his duty as man of the moment, Mr Ruttle obliged. Sally and Sheena picked up Ralph's hand and placed it in Mr Ruttle's. Realising he was holding the hand of someone important, Ralph's grip tightened.

Dennis put a large cigar in Mr Ruttle's mouth.

"Cheers, have one on me," he sniggered and struck a match.

Puffing away on the cigar and still shaking Ralph's hand, Mr Ruttle realised the train was starting to pull away.

"I really must be going," he insisted.

"But Mr Ruttle you're such a great bloke," said Dennis, patting Mr Ruttle on the back.

The train got faster.

Wrenching his hand away and diving off the train, Mr Ruttle rolled into a heap on the last half of the platform. Just as he picked himself up the cigar exploded, leaving him dishevelled but glad to be free.

Arms waving out of every carriage, laughter and the sound of "We love Ruttle's beer" faded into the distance. At the other end of the platform head brewer, George, who had travelled to the station on the other coach, was falling about laughing. Seeing his boss coming towards him he retreated down the stairs to the safety of the empty coach.

Chapter 10

Beer Festival

With only a short interlude before the major test of the day, Stuart took a walk up and down the train to see if there were any casualties. Surprisingly, there weren't. Only Ralph was showing signs of wear and tear but nobody minded that. Charlie had been filming him, amongst other things, during the trip and would have an amusing tape for the next shift. With bags and bodies intact it was now time for the assault course of entertainment: a large beer festival.

According to the literature they had been sent, it would have over 150 beers on sale, plus ciders and some foreign beers. There would be food, various stalls and attractions, including a jazz band. As it was Saturday the festival would be open all day and as the evening train wasn't departing until eight o'clock there would be plenty of time to frolic.

The guard tentatively looked on as his train was relieved of its passengers once more. He knew it would be many hours before they came back, so he must enjoy the peace. At the exit to Collingham Station a large notice said *Beer Festival 200 yards* and an arrow pointed straight ahead. Facing them was an old, 200 sq ft engine shed with noise and activity coming from it. To the right, a row of several shops. A distinctive *Oxfam* sign caught Stuart's eye.

Gathering his shift together, they let the others go on,

"Anyone fancy some unusual clothes?" Stuart asked as he pointed to the shop. Without replying they all followed Stuart and headed purposefully onwards.

It was with surprise that the small, elderly lady behind the counter viewed the crude ensemble before her. Dennis considered that an extra-large, loose-fitting summer dress would make a nice kaftan. Bruce had found a chic, emerald-coloured pill box hat with a veil. Rick had settled on a red, bell-bottomed velvet suit and a green patterned scarf. Charlie plumped for an outrageous yellow twinset and green bush hat. Other various outfits were tried on over the clothes they were wearing.

For ten minutes the shop was in utter uproar as the lads minced about in a loud manner. Eventually, almost half the contents of the shop had been tried on and purchased. The prices were so low and it was for a good cause, they told the smiling, but confused, lady serving them. She opened the door when they left, stepping outside, glad to be free of the smell of stale beer and other odours.

Half way to the festival Stuart stopped his fellow fashion leaders with,

"Did everyone get a hat?"

Stopping to look in their bags, a resounding "Yes" was the answer.

Inside the large shed, about two hundred beer devotees were enjoying the convivial atmosphere. Sally had managed to find a spare table around which she, her four friends, and a lolling Ralph sat. Looking about, they could see the stage at the far end with the toilets to the right.

Positioned around the sides of the shed were scores of silver barrels, each with various beer names and strengths written on them. Inquisitive customers scurried in and out like ants, checking the names on the barrels and then attracting the attention of the volunteer barmen.

In one corner, the food counter was also very busy and tempting aromas wafted around the building invitingly.

'Bisley Wiget', a local jazz band, were about to start their second set and warmed up enthusiastically between swigs of beer.

Upon arrival Rick, seeing the large number of barrels, felt compelled to fall to his knees and wave his outstretched arms in an act of worship. Assorted drinkers looking on found this amusing and joined in forming what looked like a dwarf Mexican wave.

"A pint of *Fossles Stench Warden*, please," requested an appreciative Jeff, glad to find a gap at the bar.

Nuzzling in behind him, other orders were given.

"I'll try a pint of *Old Foggy*," screeched Tim.

"*Old Foggy*'s gone off, Sir", the barman replied.

"Well, I hope he comes back soon," Tim broke into loud laughter and the others joined in.

Everyone got a pint then made for Sally's table just as the band started to play.

It didn't take long for the souvenir glasses to empty and with so much choice it was decided to abandon the mass round and go solo.

Being the first to finish his pint, Rick had got talking to a local man standing beside the foreign beer stand. After agreeing the beer was great and finding out the man's name was Owen, the two got into more personalised conversation.

"I'm having a trip round the world," Owen inferred, pointing to the different countries' beer bottles.

"Great idea. How far have you got? I'll join you," Rick declared.

"Well, I am a cowman by trade, so my first stop was Jersey, then France, Belgium, Holland and Germany."

Owen had a girth any festival would be proud of and, although not tall, he had a strength about him. Years of farm work had left his face red and there was a slight smell of essence de bovine.

"I'll start in Italy, then," Rick exclaimed, glad to have a beer playmate.

Near the stage Ben, cringing at the trad jazz he so loathed, was trying to get served but as there were so many people it was getting difficult. The others too were experiencing difficulty, so Bruce decided to release the pantomime horse. This horse had no costume and would be eight-legged.

Bruce took charge at the front with Roy and Alan in a line behind him. Tim was the anchorman at the back. The four started to neigh and kick one foot or hoof. Shuffling their feet, the line moved forward. Bruce shouted a beer name and they headed towards it. Amused patrons watched and parted as the route to the bar was made. On the second attempt four new "horses" were tried out with Charlie at the front, Ben and Ravi in the middle and Eugene at the rear. Gaining in confidence due to the amount of drink, they weaved and stamped and were making good progress. Reaching an unchartered part of the hall a group of about seven locals refused to budge or see the funny side of the pantomime horse. Hearing about this Stuart decided stronger tactics would be needed. Calling Juan to follow him, he quickly and quietly explained what he wanted him to do, then they headed forwards.

When Juan reached the group of locals he exclaimed,

"Ooh. Dis Inglees beer is good for de head, bad for de stomach."

The seven locals all glared at him while Stuart approached from the other side of the hall, dropped three stink bombs and walked back to Sally's table. It only took a couple of seconds before the foul, eggy, sulphurous smell parted the group. At first, they didn't realise what had caused the stench as real ale has a similar effect on the bowels.

With the beer affecting the more amorous members of the group, Dennis, Bruce and Tim decided it was time to get to know Sally's friends. Squashed up around the table, Dennis decided to break the ice,

"Anyone sitting there?" he shouted to Ros and Kathy whose shoulders were almost touching.

Before they could answer, he crawled under the table and clambered up between them, milking the laughter he got.

As Tim joined in the conversation, Bruce asked Sheena how long Ralph had been asleep and would she like him moved? The conversations were going well until Sally reached into her bag and brought out a small jar of onions, offering them round the table. All the girls took one, then another.

With their egos deflated, as well as anything else, the three lads decided it was time to dress up. Gathering the other shift members together, they headed for the men's toilets with their new outfits. Although a sign pointed the way, it was already apparent from the increasing aroma that they were going in the right direction.

Bravely venturing into the toilet, a curious sight greeted them in the end cubicle. Sprawled across the seat, trousers down over the pan, was a bearded man surrounded by a lake of regurgitated beer and food, but mostly beer. Twice the size and age of Dennis, he was snoring loudly, with his mouth wide open and his hands hanging loosely at his side. Beneath the left hand was a waterlogged walkie talkie. Just visible, on his jacket, were the words *Night security*.

"That's the lumpiest water bed I've ever seen," joked Tim.

At this point, Rick entered, en route from Poland.

"What a waste." he exclaimed seeing the beer stew all around.

It was decided to leave well alone, due to the size of the man.

Changing in a dry area of the toilet, the various strange outfits were donned and the discarded clothing put into the bags. In no time at all the group, dressed up to the nines, were trying to dance to the jazz band. Laughter broke out all around when the ordinary public were introduced to the antics of a cross between the Folies Bergère and Crufts.

Some of the band, finding it difficult to play while grinning, tried to carry on as the music floor filled up with interested patrons. Soon everyone near the stage was cutting in, wanting to dance stupidly with the flamboyant nymphets de jazz.

Juan, wearing a cape and a pointed paper hat, gave beer from a plastic watering can to anyone who could drink it the way Spanish drink sangria. Seeing the crowd were loving this he started to pretend to bullfight with loud shouts of "Olé!" as the human bulls charged his cape.

"Look at that Diego," sneered one of the locals who had not liked Juan enjoying himself earlier.

"Let's charge in," said another.

With a quick lunge, Juan was felled by five of them. Turning to see this was no accident or joke, Stuart produced a large can of avalanche foam which could travel at least six feet. After spraying it in their general direction the unhappy locals became very white.

Bruce and Charlie, reaching for their own cans, squirted them at the locals. Eugene threw a flour bomb and Ben gave them a blast with his can of fart spray. Quickly running for the door, the abominable snowmen departed, amid jeers and laughter. Thinking trouble may be starting, two sober security men rushed in but could only see scores of people dancing about to the music.

"Funny lot at this do today," said one guard.

"Yeh, but no troublemakers," said the other.

Rick had returned to Owen, his cow-herding chum, who was now in South America, or so his beer bottle stated. Somewhat bemused by Rick's attire, Owen asked,

"Did you wet yourself?"

"No, these are my travelling clothes," Rick replied.

Owen pondered on the fact that a large man who wore a red velvet flared suit and a green scarf to travel in must be very crazy but at that moment he spotted a black man with an orange beard approaching. He was wearing a yellow twinset and a bush hat. He was waving to them to go to the stage.

"Perhaps I should slow down on my beer world tour," Owen thought.

Charlie managed to get them and many others up near the stage. By now, they were all pretty drunk, but very lively, all except Ralph, who was face down on a table, fast asleep. Nearly all the revellers had accepted the fact that any objections to AMO's behaviour could have amounted to full-scale war.

A hippy leapt up on the stage. It was Jack, reeling and swaying in uncontrollable gyrations to the music. Ben took a toilet roll from his bag and swiftly hurled it but, missing Jack, scored a bullseye down the tuba instead.

Realising it was a good time to take a break, the band hurriedly finished playing and headed for the back room, instruments and beer in hand.

Stuart, feeling aggrieved that the entertainment had stopped shouted,

"Haka, Haka," and stepped up onto the stage.

He was joined by Dennis, Tim, Charlie, Bruce, Jeff, Eugene, Barry, Roy and Alan. At the back of the stage Jack was still dancing. Getting into formation, with Stuart at the front, they re-enacted the start of the New Zealand rugby team's famous tribal challenge. Of course, they had done this many times in the past and were well practised. Loudly and strongly they chanted but, due to their Oxfam clothing, false beards, breasts, ears, and staggered manner, the war cries were not quite as authentic as the genuine Kiwis'.

A loud cheer rang out when they had finished. They bowed briefly before starting the last number of their set. Arms bent and flapping, mouths clucking, the chicken cancan was next. At one point the stage creaked under the strain of the French chickens pretending to do the splits and raising their backsides in the air. Dennis got the best laugh as he was wearing his loose kaftan/summer dress with a huge plastic bottom underneath.

With the addition of several metres of plastic string, streamers, and shaving foam, the gallant band stepped down from the stage looking like the leftovers from a hoedown on Mars.

~~~~~~~~~~~~

Meanwhile, back on the train, the guard, grinning wildly put the top back on a bottle of re-cycled railway bitter. He knew he would only get his own back on a few of them but it would be worth it. As beer bottles were usually brown, no-one would notice he had urinated inside and put them back into the crate for re-sale.

Some of the more drunken passengers had started to board the train, unable to resist the urge to sleep any longer. Around the station, activity would start to increase over the next couple of hours.

~~~~~~~~~~~~

Back at the foreign beer stand, Australia had been reached.

"Cheers, Cobber," a swaying Rick gestured to Owen, beer in hand, who belched and replied,

"I'm getting jet lag."

With only two hours to go until the train departed, Stuart decided it was time to go and have some fun in the market town. As word got around, a slow procession started to head for the outside world once more.

Owen informed Rick he was off to round up his herd of cows. Rick, wondering at the wisdom of this move, shook his hand and said,

"Good travelling with you. All the best mate."

Sally and friends picked Ralph up and decided it was time to start some fun of their own. After getting the unconscious Ralph outside they undressed him and swapped his clothes for a short-sleeved gingham checked mini dress. Sally then ran to the phone box at the station and reported a drunken streaker at the beer festival. Having diverted the police attention for a while, the motley crew headed for a nearby carnival. Two local cub packs were on a float waving to the crowd lining the street. Stuart saw his chance.

"This way lads," he shouted to the rest of the group and they all boarded the float with the cubs, scurrying up to one end.

A variety of false beards, hats, dresses, and assorted novelty items were donned and then the waving to the crowd began. Not knowing any better, the public responded and cheered and waved back. Basking in the glory, a volley of foam, streamers, and plastic string was sprayed into the spectators.

At the station the entrance had been blocked and two very young but over-zealous station employees were checking the tickets back to Kings Cross. The queue was getting longer so Stuart decided to organize the troops of the 1st Buffoons for some manoeuvres as they now needed to use the toilets urgently.

The computer operators got into a huddle, Stuart whispered his orders and an attack formation was taken up. The order "proceed" was given by Stuart and the first wave of smoke bombs was thrown. As the yellow, blue and red smoke billowed about, a batch of distraction rocket balloons was quickly inflated and launched in several directions. A split second after that a sea of avalanche foam was released towards the obstructive train staff and stink bombs landed near their feet.

From the back of the queue other drinkers had been handed weapons. Stuart then called out,

"Flour brigade, Fire. Water brigade, Fire." and dozens of flour bombs and water bombs were propelled to the combat zone with devastating consequences.

While the battle was raging, ten potato guns peppered pellets into the locality, followed by toy parachute men that were thrown up in the air and left to float down on the bemused train staff. Flying disc guns sent spinning discs around and over their heads.

Seconds later the order to charge was given and around fifty drunken comedy soldiers, ran and staggered and shouted AAARRRGGGHHH as they broke the enemy's resolve and advanced down the stairs. This daring raid would go down in drunken rambling circles as the 'Battle of Bulging Bladder'.

Once on the train, Tim and Jeff were seated next to each other. The day's beer was taking its toll and they started to nod off. Charlie and Dennis had been watching them from the platform and it was only a matter of seconds before Tim and Jeff were fast asleep. Charlie had saved an orange in his bag and, creeping up to the open train window, threw it in at Tim, scoring a direct hit on his forehead, Tim woke with a start, swore at Jeff and punched him in the face. Jeff woke up, swore at Tim and punched *him* in the face.

Charlie and Dennis were laughing loudly as they ran into the carriage to prevent a scrap. They explained to Tim and Jeff that someone had run past and lobbed an orange in at them. On finding the offending article on the train floor, peace was restored, for a while, at least.

Gradually the train filled up with increasing noise. Two local press reporters started to take pictures for an amusing report to brighten up their paper. If only they hadn't boarded the train all would have been fine.

They managed to take quite a few pictures before they were jumped on and wrapped in large rolls of Sellotape from neck to toe. After being liberally doused with fart spray, foam, eggs, and flour, they were then secured together on two empty seats and left, wriggling like maggots, under a large pile of coats, mumbling into their gags.

Rick had been watching discreetly at the station entrance as the train staff continued to clear up the detritus left over from the Battle of Bulging Bladder. On seeing a police car arrive he feared the worst but could see they were looking at him so he approached the car.

"Everything all right, officer?" Rick gingerly asked.

"Is this the train going back to London with the Sulcrem House lot?" the officer enquired.

"Yes, it is," Rick replied, fingers crossed.

Beckoning him to the car, the officer said,

"Follow me please Sir."

Rick walked with him to the waiting police car from where two other officers emerged. Inside the car was the lolling figure of a short-haired man in a gingham checked dress and nothing else.

"Do you know this person sir?" asked the officer.

Rick looked in the vehicle and said,

"Yes, this is department manager Ralph Parkett."

The other officers chuckled. They eased Ralph out of the car and told Rick he had been lucky this time.

Not noticing the breeze blowing his skirt up, Gingham girl, eyes slowly surveying his surroundings, gasped,

"Where am I?"

The first officer directed,

"Get him back home quickly."

Rick put his arm round Ralph and slowly walked him to the train where dozens of laughing faces whistled and shouted,

"When's the wedding?"

As he sat down heavily, Ralph looked down and noticed his bare legs for the first time. He raised the hem of the dress and looked bewildered. The guard appeared and quickly handed Ralph a bottle of railway bitter. The guard had reached the end of the carriage when a sickly cry, coupled with a spraying and spitting sound, covered all who sat in Ralph's vicinity. Heading back to the sanctuary of his compartment, the guard smirked as the bottle of urine was debated upon.

Fifteen minutes later, as the train gradually started to pull away from the station, Roy and Alan were grabbing at each other's throats. The passengers on the opposite platform stared askance as Roy produced a trick knife and pretended to stab Alan in the neck. Alan went down and in a split second had burst the fake blood bag he had brought and it was all over the top of his shirt. He then started shouting to the passengers opposite "Help me." A woman screamed and dozens of pairs of eyes widely watched what was happening. Roy then started throwing fake plastic fingers from the train window with Alan holding a closed fist covered in fake blood.

As they slowly moved out of sight, in the next carriage Juan and Barry had been munching joke blue mouth sweets and they poked their tongues out as the train passed by the already shocked passengers. Thinking there was nothing else left to alarm them, the passengers were then greeted by the sight of Greg in the last carriage, jeans down with a twelve-inch fake penis lodged at the top of his pants. Brian was throwing plastic rings over the penis shouting "Hoop La," loudly every time one landed correctly.

The train slowly proceeded down the track leaving behind a platform full of smoke bombs, stink bombs, silly string foam, flour, and a bottle of urine. No one had yet discovered the two reporters who were now heading southward.

Ralph sat, head in hands, feeling about as low as anyone could be, wondering just how he was going to get home in a dress.

Back at the station a relieved train staff hosed down the platform pondering on what had just happened.

As the train slowly proceeded forward Jeff made a small circle over his eyes with the thumb and index finger of each hand. By upturning his wrists the rest of his fingers stretched down the side of his face like a pretend 1940s airman's helmet. He started to hum the Dambusters' tune. Everyone immediately joined in and within seconds the sound reached a crescendo throughout the carriages.

About two hundred yards down the track the train screeched to a halt as a stocky, red faced man swore and ran to and fro waving at several dozen cows. As the track cleared and the train rolled on, Rick recognised his beer buddy, Owen, drunkenly staggering after his herd as it scattered in all directions towards the town.

Chapter 11

Homeward Bound

Thirty minutes had gone by since the train departed from Collingham Station and the headache season had started. After eating all their remaining rolls and snacks and finally slowing down in the proceedings, the day's drinking was taking its toll.

In Sally's carriage they were still talking and eating onions and it had become a no go area. Rick decided to lend Ralph his flared velvet suit. As the trousers were so big he had sellotaped the waist and the flares. Eugene lent him a tank top and Charlie his green bush hat. Ralph felt stupid but was delighted to be out of the gingham dress.

Beer was still being drunk, but at a much slower pace. Another minor victory for the guard occurred when Rick had spluttered on the railway bitter, insisting he had tasted worse, but not venturing another swig.

Forty miles from Collingham the two reporters were discovered so the driver had radioed ahead and it was arranged to drop them off at the next station. They could have summoned the police but were relieved to be free at last. As the train stopped briefly to liberate the reporters, Bruce, Barry and Tim planned a daring raid.

A sack barrow containing two bags of manure stood at one end of the station. Swiftly they got out, grabbed the bags of manure, then the barrow and wrestled them onto the train. Some of the local gardeners would be deprived of fertilizer, but more importantly, another prank could now be played.

As Gordon from the day shift fell victim to the last bottle of railway bitter, it was decided it was the guard who had doctored the beer and he would have to pay. Braving the stench of onions, Stuart went to the girls' carriage and asked them if they would mind coaxing the guard out from his small compartment. Knowing something funny was about to happen they obliged.

Giving an excuse about feeling faint Sally fell against the guard as he half hid behind the door. Feeling concerned, he helped her to sit down. After a few minutes she thanked him and started to go back, to her friends. Unfortunately for the guard the way to his own compartment was now blocked by what seemed to him like a very rough looking bunch.

A scraping and clunking could be heard coming from the aisle. Bruce, Barry and Tim approached with the barrow which they duly put in the middle of the aisle outside the guard's van.

"Grab him lads," bellowed Stuart and they charged from both ends.

Within minutes the experts had mummified him with the very handy thick Sellotape they liked to use.

They manouvered the guard on to the barrow and sellotaped him to it. His startled eyes watched as he hoped nothing else would happen.

"Can we put this lot on him now?" inquired Eugene, holding up one of the bags of horse muck.

"Carry on," directed Stuart.

The bags of fertilizer were liberally dispersed over the barrow and the stinking quivering mass was left to fester.

"You'll be a foot taller by the time we get to London."

Charlie's video collection had increased greatly during the day and it was amazing the camera was still in one piece. He took a slow shot of several sleeping beer ramblers and, panning down, the sea of debris and gunge on the floor.

According to Stuart's calculations, there were only about thirty minutes remaining of the train journey so he decided to try and get everyone going again with a chant. Standing up he yelled,

"Curry house," and clapped his hands three times in short succession.

Everyone in the carriage joined in at once, so did the members of the next carriage, although not as enthusiastically. Stuart had now put the thought in everyone's mind and the AMO body abuse club would try the final phase on arrival – a nice hot curry.

During the next twenty minutes Jeff entertained with a collection of Spurs' football songs, while Charlie, putting the video camera down for once, did a good impression of an American soul singer. Eugene tried a couple of Chas 'n' Dave hits but was pelted with anything available and had to stop.

The highlight of the impromptu concert was Juan doing his version of Julio Iglesias and he bowed as people clapped and shouted "more." Ravi decided what was needed was an Indian theme and stood up to sing a rendition of 'Land of Hope and Glory' in a Bombay accent. By now everyone was back in the swing of things and finished up with "Meet the gang 'cos the boys are here, the boys to entertain you", the theme tune 'from the popular television series, *It Ain't Half Hot, Mum.*

As the train reached its destination, all the windows were down and several heads popped out to cheer at the sight of the London station. Some of the lads gathered together their remaining belongings, while the others threw smoke bombs and flour on to the platform. After a mass drunken sprint through the barrier the main body of men and women assembled on the street. Ralph decided that safety in numbers was best and he could phone a taxi from the curry house, so he kept up with them all.

When the coloured smoke had cleared, a lone railway inspector looked at the platform and then boarded the deserted train. On the floor eggs, flour, foam, beer, straw, fertilizer, plastic broken bottoms, beards with plastic string hanging off, a range of women's clothing, toilet rolls, and many metres of Sellotape met his gaze.

Walking down the train, fighting his way through the mess, he eventually discovered a railway guard under a pile of the most putrid muck he had ever smelled. Shell-shocked, he stepped back onto the platform and stared, wide-eyed, mouth open, almost disbelieving the sight that had befallen him. Not sure where to start, he thought the guard would need releasing first so, shaking his head in disbelief, he re-boarded the train.

~~~~~~~~~~~~~~~~

Three streets away the large Indian restaurant was trying to seat the large party that had just arrived. Seeing the state they were in, the other patrons hurried to finish their meals and leave.

After the obligatory pint of lager while they waited, various curries were ordered. The waiters knew most of the crowd as they were regular customers. They also knew that although all of the meals wouldn't be finished, a good tip would still follow.

Ravi went round with a tea towel on his head taking fake orders in his best Indian accent. He shouted to the real waiters,

"Ranjid, throw this one out, he is much trouble," pointing to Eugene.

Barry tried to explain to Juan about curry as he had never had it before.

"You need to start with a mild one so it won't burn you," Juan nodded.

"OK, which one I have, Barry?"

Pointing to the right side of the menu, with his fingers over the words 'very hot', Barry advised,

"Vindaloo is what you want."

As the starter course arrived, word soon got round that the girls were all having onion bhajis.

In no time at all the plates were cleared and everyone thought they had plenty of room for more but, halfway through the main course, it was a different story.

Charlie had left his seat to film Juan who was going red, sweating, eyes watering, nose running, and occasionally hiccupping. He didn't want to appear weak to Barry who had recommended what he had.

"Barry, how come you ok?" Juan queried.

"Oh, don't worry, you'll soon be on the hot ones after a while," Barry enthused.

Juan tried to carry on and thought,

"These Inglees can eat anything."

On finishing the obligatory ice cream, Jack started dancing to the Eastern music which was playing in the background, the amount he had drunk, impairing his thought processes.

Stuart asked for a doggy bag for the leftovers. The bag was completely filled. What Eugene hadn't realised was that he had been voted leftover man by the lads. A title not easily dispensed. On leaving the restaurant, Eugene was seized abruptly. A convenient lamp post with a bin on one side, would hold Eugene as he was secured by the famous Sellotape. Stuart made a modest speech along the lines of

"For his services to stupidity etc., etc."

The bag of leftovers was then introduced to Eugene's head, the sauce running down his face and neck and pieces of rice sticking to him. A loud cheer rang out and Eugene was left shrieking obscenities as the taxis arrived.

After a good night's sleep with the odd interruption for the toilet, most of the group would be reasonable again. Although chaos had been caused there were no arrests –

just, and no fights. It only remained to find out whether Ralph would ban everyone from attending another outing ever again.

Fortunately for them all, Ralph couldn't remember much about what had happened. He spent the whole of the next day in bed recovering. Stuart led a small party to *The Tardis* for a lunchtime pick-me-up and tales were told of their adventures to the bar staff.

Eugene's mum looked at the state of him when he got home and barred him from going out with his workmates for a month. She was still fuming about the taxi driver's remark,

"Does this belong to you?" as he had pointed to her son.

Juan returned home to tell his family they should never eat that devil food curry.

The girls all went back to Sally's for a coffee without onions.

Chapter 12

Management Stress

On Monday, Stuart's shift was on days and Ralph was due to give a seminar on the correct procedures to follow at work. A video and television stood in the large conference room and Ralph's flip chart awaited his felt pen. Everyone looked smart in shirts and ties, clean shaven, going about the daily routines of a computer department.

Sally smiled as she greeted the fifty or so middle managers and assistants who had arrived for Ralph's course. She pressed Ralph's number on the intercom and in her most official voice said,

"Mr Parkett, your course members have arrived."

After a pause, an even more official reply came,

"I'll be right out, thank you."

Through the double doors a few seconds later, Ralph greeted his guests, dressed immaculately in his three-piece suit. He walked over to them and spoke as if he were the king holding court for the lucky few. After a while he beckoned them upstairs to the conference room where tea and coffee were waiting.

While they were drinking Ralph turned the television on to video mode and started to check his agenda at a desk at the front of the room. Anyone attending would have been impressed by his totally professional manner as he spoke about correct procedure being the most important thing in the computer revolution.

Introducing the first video he explained it would show how he had changed the image of management at Sulcrem House. As the lights were switched off and the video pressed to 'play' the picture on the screen showed a railway station and Ralph in a gingham checked mini dress, with Rick's arm around him staggering to board the train.

A small giggle turned to loud laughter. The room shook with humour.

Charlie had been asked to set up the video recorder beforehand and had switched the tapes. It would also not be long before the laxative tablets in the tea and coffee started to work. All this had taken Charlie a matter of a couple of minutes but it would severely disrupt the day's course.

Sally watched, trying not to grin as Ralph escorted the first few attendees to the toilets.

This was a procedure that would become very monotonous as the morning wore on. It was decided to abandon the course until everyone had recovered from the mystery illness. Ralph called all of Stuart's shift to his office and gave them a warning about behaviour. Once again, he could not prove anything and it had been him dressed in gingham so he didn't go too hard on them.

With half of the shift going to the Sulcrem House bar at lunchtime an orderly stillness came over the computer department. Charlie gave his tape of the Lincoln trip a viewing to the rest of the lads. When those who had gone to the bar first returned, he played it to them.

Loud laughter could be heard coming from the rest room, but then, that was normal thought Ivan, on his rounds and sober this time. He peeked through the glass in the door just as the video showed Ralph wearing the gingham dress. Watching on he saw the two reporters being tied up. By the time the train guard was being covered in fertilizer, Ivan roared with laughter.

Opening the door, he asked to see the rest of the video and he was warmly welcomed into the room. Rick went and got him four bottles of strong bitter from his locker.

"No hard feelings?" he coaxed as Ivan looked at the beer.

"I don't know how you buggers get away with it. No hard feelings lads," signed Ivan, taking the beer.

"Drink it at home this time Ivan," sniped Eugene.

"I will, don't you worry."

On saying this, Ivan rose and walked, chuckling, back to his security hut.

At 3.15 the evening shift, led by Keith, strolled in and various expletives were exchanged. The talk was mostly of Ralph's failed course and a few words of what work needed to be done during the coming evening. Jack, the cleaner, was still trying to clear up in the toilets and replace the empty toilet rolls.

In the car park two motorbikes from the evening shift had been padlocked together and pieces of cactus superglued to the seats. A notice on the padlock read *Keys in reception*. Rick had been busy indulging in inter-shift sabotage again. He hadn't forgiven them for jamming his locker with a broken key on the last shift.

Interrupting the march from the computer room, Stuart remarked,

"Anyone fancy *The Tardis* tonight?"

A silence for a moment, then Rick replied,

"I'll go."

The rest slowly agreed and, being very well paid, did not worry about the expense of Monday night drinking. After ten years of this lifestyle the lads had become accustomed to the pursuit of pleasure whenever they could.

That evening, Charlie gave the landlord the tape of the Lincoln trip and he played it back to the pub. Once again, the atmosphere was a happy one and even their girlfriends laughed at what they saw.

At one end of the bar, Rick turned to Stuart and sighed,
"It won't always be like this you know?"
Pausing only to grin Stuart replied,
"You wanna bet?"